# Readers love
# I'm Somebody Too

Simply wonderful!
—*Richard Wainwright, Family Life Publications*

A beautiful story, full of heart knowledge, simply and
sparsely told. The imagery is at once lovely and
painful, the language true.
—*Wilma Fessenden, MSLS, New York*

A fascinating picture of how a child's mind and emotions
work under stress. I enjoyed the book so much that I
couldn't put it down until the last page.
—*Laurie Pratts, Colorado*

Engaging, lively characters.
—*Kathleen M. Muldoon, author of*
***Princess Pooh,*** *Texas*

I was continually struck by similarities between
families coping with ADD members and those coping
with alcoholics. There is no better way than ***I'm***
***Somebody Too*** to help understand  the feelings of a
sibling who feels left out and alone.
—*Evelyn Petersen, "Parent Talk," Detroit Free Press*

This is a very good book about a girl and her family and
friends.  I liked it and I hope you will too.
—*Naomi, age 8*

# I'm Somebody Too

JEANNE GEHRET

**Verbal Images Press**
Fairport, New York

ISBN 09625136-6-0 paperback
ISBN 09625136-7-9 hardcover

Copyright © 1992 by Jeanne Gehret

Printed in Mexico

**Publisher's Cataloging in Publication**

Gehret, Jeanne, 1953-
    I'm somebody too / by Jeanne Gehret.
    p. cm.
    Audience: Ages 9 and up.
    ISBN 0-9625136-7-9 (cloth)
    ISBN 0-9625136-6-0 (pbk.)

    1. Exceptional children—Juvenile fiction.  2. Attention deficit disorders—Juvenile fiction.  3. Sibling rivalry—Juvenile fiction.
I. Title.

RJ496.A86G4 1992        618.928'589
                        QBI92-10610

**Verbal Images Press**
19 Fox Hill Drive • Fairport, New York 14450
(716) 377-3807 • Fax (716) 377-5401

*Grateful acknowledgments to:*

Helen and Ed Barton, Eleanor Celentani, Ceil Goldman, Cary Hull, Nanette Levin, Rebecca Wood, and many others who encouraged me as I wrote this book. Special hugs to Emily and to Jon and Danny Gehret.

*For Elizabeth,*
*my inspiration*

# Prologue

The spring I was almost twelve, no one needed me. My best friend Ginny started hanging around with another bunch of girls, and my parents were so wrapped up in my brother that they hardly realized I was alive.

I always envied families that did fun things together and had kids who were close. My family was not like that at the beginning. In fact, until that spring, life with Ben and my parents was full of tension and sadness. Now, many years later, I understand that we were battling silently with a problem we couldn't even name.

Ben and I have talked about our turning point many times. To hear him tell it, I was just as mixed up as he was before then. He insists that I was far from the model child I pretended to be. I guess I never fooled him, but then, what would you expect from a brother whose nickname was Eagle Eyes?

When he tells this story, he's the hero and I'm the villain. When you hear my version, however, maybe you'll think a little more kindly of the girl I really was.

§§§

# I'm Somebody Too

# Chapter 1

Back then I thought I had to be perfect. My brother, Ben, needed lots of help and flubbed up so often, I figured it was my job to make up for all the grief he gave Mom and Dad. The funny thing was, though, that the harder I tried, the less I succeeded in pleasing anyone — especially myself.

One day in January, my mother really let Ben have it. As usual, it was an awful morning at our house. I had gotten dressed and was heading downstairs when Mom went into my eight-year-old brother's room. "Good morning, Ben," she said, opening his door. "How are you this bright..." She interrupted herself. "What's that on your rug?"

Silence.

"Ben, it looks like paint. What have you done?"

He mumbled something I couldn't hear.

"Ben, paint won't come off of rugs," Mom continued. "Whatever were you thinking of, painting on your rug?"

"I didn't mean it," he mumbled. "How come you let Emily use paint wherever she wants to?"

# I'm Somebody Too

"Emily is three years older than you, and she uses it in the kitchen on top of lots of newspapers. Give me the paint."

"But I want to finish my model airplane," he said, his voice rising. "Can't I just keep it till I'm done?"

Mom's voice grew insistent. "Give me the paint right now, Ben, and finish getting dressed. You should be making your lunch by now."

Suddenly I remembered that I had not packed my lunch yet, so I hurried to finish it right away. Then Mom would see that at least one of us did what we were supposed to do, and her frown would disappear.

"Morning, Mom," I said cheerfully when she padded into the kitchen in her slippers. She never wore shoes unless she had to. "Would you like me to fix you some tea?"

"Yes, honey." As she turned to me, I was happy to see her green eyes soften and the crease disappear from between her brows. "That would be nice. Have you made your lunch yet?"

"In my backpack," I assured her, waiting for her to tell me what a good job I'd done. Instead, she looked at her watch and strode to the bottom of the stairs.

"Ben, you need to come down and make your lunch," Mom repeated firmly. Suddenly he bounded out of his room and half-ran, half-slid down the stairs. "Ben, watch your step!" Mom cautioned. "You could slip," she added lamely, for he was already at the bottom of the staircase.

# I'm Somebody Too

Mom surveyed Ben carefully. His wavy blond hair was uncombed, but she must have decided to let that go when she saw the rest of him. "You can't wear those pants; they're full of paint! Oh, Ben, those were new school pants! How will we get it off?" She took a deep breath as if to control herself. "Go change right now."

Any other kid would have recognized how much trouble he was in and hurried to do what Mom asked — but not Ben. He argued about changing his pants, then took his time fixing breakfast. He dawdled over his cereal, dripping milk all over the place. Mom hardly looked at either of us; she didn't even drink her tea or sit down. I think she was trying very hard to hold her temper.

Suddenly I noticed the clock and jumped up. "Oh, it's eight-fifteen!" I exclaimed. That's when we're supposed to leave to catch our bus. Pulling my hat down over my brown hair, I jammed my arms into my coat sleeves and grabbed my backpack.

"Let's go, Ben," I said, heading toward the front door.

"I can't find my coat," he reported. Mom started rummaging through the closet. "If you'd hang your coat up instead of dropping it on the floor, it would be much easier to find," she grumbled. "Emily, please see if it's in the car."

As I returned empty-handed, I heard the unmistakable rumble of the school bus as it sped up the hill past our house. "Mom, there goes the bus," I said, hating to report the bad news to her.

Mom's arms were full of Ben's fall sweatshirts and jackets. Sighing loudly, she dropped them all to the closet floor. "Darn it, Ben, I don't have TIME to take you to school this morning," she shrilled. "I'll be late for my meeting." The big crease between her eyebrows returned.

*Say you're sorry, Ben,* I pleaded silently, *before she gets really mad.* But he just stood there tossing his hat in the air and catching it. Then something inside her seemed to snap.

"Ben, get your coat and backpack and LET'S GO!" she yelled, giving him a little shove.

"How *can* I get it? I don't know where it is!" he yelled back. I got into the car so I wouldn't have to listen to the rest. But I didn't really have a choice, because Mom yelled at Ben most of the way to Northwood School, stopping just long enough to give each of us a kiss before she drove away.

When I was almost at the door of the building, a bus pulled in front of school and my best friend, Ginny, jumped down from the high step. "Emily, where were you this morning?" she called, her soft blonde hair peeping out from under her hood.

"Ben couldn't find his coat and we missed the bus," I replied, looking at her. "Mom was really mad."

In the ten years that we had been best friends, Ginny had hung around our house often enough to know how Mom acted when she'd lost it. Her blue eyes clouded with sympathy. "You poor thing. Did he ever find it?"

"No, and he was supposed to check in the Lost and Found, but I'd better do it in case he forgets. Want to come along?"

"Sure," she said, falling into step next to me. "You know that girl Melissa who's new on our bus? She was in chorus yesterday. She sat in the last row of sopranos." Searching my memory for her face, I pictured the music room, with the girls who had high voices (sopranos) sitting in front. I sat behind them with the altos, who had lower voices. In the back of the room sat all the boys; our music teacher called them tenors.

I nodded without comment. Ginny had a high, true voice and could remember a tune the first time she'd heard it. But I found my alto parts hard to learn and dull to sing. If only we got to carry the tune more often, I thought, there would be some sense to it. To me chorus was an ordeal; to Ginny it was fun. It was about the only thing we disagreed on.

That afternoon I dreaded seeing Mom's face when she learned that Ben's coat hadn't turned up. Hoping to soften the blow, I ran up the hill ahead of him to our old three-story house. Mom's keys and purse were on the hall table. She greeted me in stockinged feet, still wearing her skirt and blouse from her job at the library. Her brown bangs just brushed her eyebrows, and her smooth hair turned under gently at her shoulders. Dad often praised her slender figure in front of other people, and she would say, "Oh, Larry," blushing a little. I was proud of her, too, and wondered if my squarish face would ever be as softly rounded as hers.

Although I was almost twelve, I still loved to hug her and bury my face in her fragrant hair. She broke away from me, however, when Ben burst through the door. Flinging his backpack on the floor, he headed for the bathroom without even shutting the door. "Hi, Ben," she called after him.

I was grateful when she seemed to accept the news about his coat calmly. Later, when I was alone in my room, I found out how she really felt. Ben was finally asleep, having been tucked in over and over for almost an hour. The house was so quiet that Mom's voice rose clearly through the floor register from the living room below, where she sat with Dad.

"We had an awful morning again," she began, and told him all about the coat. He let her talk until her voice began to rise, then he interrupted. "Nell, you just have to be stricter with the boy. When *I* tell him to do something, he does it right away."

"Well, maybe that's because you're hardly ever here," she said hotly. "And when you are home, you're always doing your own thing. No wonder he pays attention when you tell him to do something — he's polite because you're like a stranger!"

"Nell, what I do with my time is not the issue here," he said, sounding very calm. "We were talking about how you discipline him when you're here. And I think you need to be stricter." His voice softened. "Don't get me wrong; I appreciate all that you do. I'm just trying to help." After that, he launched into a description of some of the birds he had photographed last week.

A few evenings later, when I tuned in to their nightly conversation, Mom was very excited. "Larry, I was telling one of the other librarians about Ben and he said it sounds exactly like his son. They found out he has..." The blower of the furnace came on, and for the next few minutes I couldn't hear a thing. Even when it stopped, however, Mom was speaking so quietly I could hardly hear her.

Dad replied, "Ben can't have..." I couldn't make out what he was saying. I shuddered, imagining all sorts of nameless diseases. "That's a mental illness," he continued. "Ben's not mentally ill; he's just stubborn and undisciplined and..."

Mom broke in again. "It *isn't* a mental illness, but it is a problem in the brain. John says his son's brain doesn't do a very good job of controlling how he moves and thinks. He talks constantly and forgets things and doesn't do what they ask. But when they give him medicine, he's much better."

"What kind of medicine?" Dad wanted to know.

"Something called Ritalin. It slows him down and makes him easier to get along with."

"Ritalin! Isn't that a very strong drug? I've heard

of kids who were on Ritalin and they went around with their eyes glazed."

Mom laughed bitterly — a short sarcastic sound that was more like a cough. I hated that sound because I could still remember the beautiful way she used to giggle when I was small.

"Just what I want — a compliant zombie," she replied to Dad in the same sarcastic way. "Why can't Ben be just a normal kid like Emily? She's so sweet and she always does what she's supposed to do. I don't know what I'd do without her."

I could hardly believe my ears: Mom so rarely said anything nice to me. *I'll never let you down, Mom,* I thought, my heart swelling with love for her. *I will be so helpful and such a good student that I'll make you forget all about whatever is wrong with Ben.*

*But what* is *wrong with Ben?*

# Chapter 2

I thought chorus would never end. From the tenor section, Robbie Johnson threw spitballs at Ginny. He was crazy about her, but she didn't care. She told me he was ugly and skinny next to her idol Joe Haze, who played electric piano for her favorite band, The Stranger.

Toward the end of activity period, our music teacher, Mr. Renfro, worked a lot with us altos. Over and over he made us repeat the same boring phrase until we got it right. The tenors snickered and bumped their unpadded theater seats, making it hard for me to hear the teacher's directions. Suddenly a spitball hit Mr. Renfro right next to his ear.

A mild-mannered man who loved music, Mr. Renfro hardly ever raised his voice, even when we were not doing what he wanted. Sometimes his classes really got out of hand. I felt bad for him, even though he was too fussy about music, about how he dressed, about everything.

Brushing the spitball off his face, he told the tenors to stay after and dismissed the rest of us.

"Whew!" I said to Ginny once we were partway

down the hall. "Robbie Johnson would've been dead if he had done that in Mr. Miller's class!" She nodded in agreement.

"Oh, look! The sun is shining," I continued. "Do you want to go for a bike ride when we get home, Ginny?"

It was an unusually beautiful day for January in Penfield, New York, where we lived. January, February, and March brought a long series of snowfalls and thaws. Mom and Dad said that Lake Ontario, only five miles north of us, was somehow responsible for the gray skies that started in November and lasted until about April. Today, however, was one of those sunny, warm days that I loved. It felt like spring might break loose any minute, even though I knew that true spring weather was at least three months away.

Before Ginny could answer, the new girl, Melissa, called, "Ginny, wait up!" Running to catch up with us, Melissa said somewhat breathlessly, "You were going to come over to hear my new Stranger album after school, remember?"

So that's what they were whispering about in the soprano section while I was rehearsing that dumb song with the altos. Glancing sideways at Ginny, I saw her face light up for a moment; but then she noticed me looking.

"Um, sure," she said. "Can Emily come along too?"

"Okay," said Melissa. She sounded a little reluctant to me. "Boy, I thought you altos would never get your part. That's such an easy song."

As she sang the melody in a voice as beautiful as Ginny's, I looked at her enviously. Her long curly hair was an unusual color — rich dark brown with red in it — and she wore it pulled back with a barrette that had fancy ribbons flowing from it. Beneath her open jacket she wore a bright new sweater with bows all over — the kind Mom always refused to buy me because she said it would go out of style too soon.

Ginny joined her on the chorus, pausing to urge, "Emily, sing your part." I shook my head; I didn't know it well enough yet, and next to two perfect sopranos I would really sound bad.

During the whole trip home they sang, discovering one song after another that they both liked. We were sitting three in a seat, with Melissa in first, then Ginny. I was hanging off halfway into the aisle, and every time the bus rounded a corner, I almost tumbled off. When we finally reached our stop, I was glad to get up. Ben was hurrying toward the door when I noticed his backpack in the seat.

"Ben, your backpack!" I called. Mine was heavy enough, but his felt like it had rocks in it. As I struggled to lift it into the aisle, people behind me were getting restless.

"Is he your *brother*?" Melissa asked, her lips curling in distaste. I nodded, nervous about what she would say next. Did she know him?

"I saw him sitting in the hall when I took the

attendance to the office," she said, flipping a curl over her shoulder.

*Uh-oh,* I thought. *What's he done now?*

"Hurry up, Emily. People are waiting," Melissa said, settling back in the seat for the rest of her bus ride. Ginny took one strap of Ben's backpack and helped me down the aisle.

"See you in a few minutes?" Melissa called.

"Okay, I just have to call my mom at work and let her know I'm home," Ginny called back, then looked inquiringly at me.

"Uh, I don't think my mom will let me," I lied. "Maybe next time." I headed up the hill toward home.

Last week's snowfall had melted away, leaving the grass matted down and dull brown. Behind the houses across the street lay a golf course where crows were calling loudly to each other.

The warm breeze made my winter coat feel bulky and hot. Suddenly I realized that I was carrying Ben's two-ton load.

"Ben, come get your backpack," I yelled ahead to him. He kept walking up the hill as if he hadn't heard.

"I'm going to leave it right here, Ben, and you come get it." Setting his stuff down made me feel so light that I began to run.

"Wait up," Ginny said, panting behind me. "I'm sorry I can't come for a bike ride with you. Are you sure you won't come to Melissa's instead?"

"No, that's okay," I said, avoiding her eyes. After

having a quick snack at home, I went for a bike ride by myself and tried not to miss Ginny.

Dad hummed "Turkey in the Straw" while he was doing supper dishes, then settled into his usual spot on the couch to watch the news. I could almost always find Dad in one of his two favorite places: on the couch or in his bathroom "darkroom" developing photographs he took. A tall, muscular man with a beard, he usually smelled of the outdoors — that is, when he didn't smell of darkroom chemicals.

Mom was following her evening routine, too, when she told us, "Get your backpacks, kids, and see what you have for homework." I started right to work studying for my test of all the states in the United States. Mr. Miller, our teacher, had given us a blank map to practice on, and I was able to fill in thirty without looking once. At this rate I would be done with homework in time to try a French braid in my hair.

Ben was hopping from one foot to the other, humming. "Ben, where's your backpack?" Mom repeated. Whenever she wanted Ben to do something, she always had to ask him several times.

"I don't know," he replied, still hopping. "Oh, Emily had it. Emily, where's my backpack?"

As if in a movie, I saw myself laying it down by the sidewalk and scampering up the hill. "I laid it down in front of the Pattersons' house. And I called you to come get it, remember?"

Ben stood still so suddenly that the effect was

jarring. "I didn't hear you," he said defensively.

"Well, you should have, but you just kept walking. Melissa wanted to know why you're such a creep."

"Emily, there was a very important note from Ben's teacher in his backpack. She just called. How could you leave it like that?" Mom said crossly. She frowned at me for calling Ben a name.

She hardly ever looked at or spoke to me that way, and I didn't like it. Suddenly all the things I would have said in my own defense seemed unimportant. "I'll go get it, Mom," I said quietly. Ben shot me a triumphant look. I made a face back.

Mom saw it. "Emily!" Before she could scold me further, I grabbed my coat and went out into the night.

It was raining, but I hardly cared. The cold drops almost felt good on my hot face. All the angry words went round and round inside my head like an awful record. *Ben never listens except when he wants to! Besides, how could I know about the note? It wasn't even my backpack. If it hadn't been for me, it would still be on the bus, where he left it. Next time I'll just leave it there!*

Depositing the backpack at Ben's feet without a word, I went upstairs and got ready for bed. Mom must have gotten busy helping Ben with homework, because she forgot to kiss me goodnight.

Before dawn I woke feeling hot, with a scratchy throat. My tangled blankets pinned me to the bed. It had taken me a long time to fall asleep, and then I had seen my own angry face in the dream saying terrible things to Mom. The worst part, though, is that she looked right through me as if I weren't there.

After waking, I discovered that I'd been holding my breath, so I slowly let it out and looked around my room. It was still so dark I had to imagine my beautiful blue walls, which were the exact shade of the summer sky. Last year Mom had made me a white eyelet bedspread and curtains to replace the Minnie Mouse set I'd had since I was three. Opposite my bed on the closet door hung a poster of a white unicorn racing through a field of flowers, and my American Girls books were lined up neatly on the shelf next to my bed. I was proud of my room and usually kept it picked up so I could see the things I loved.

This morning, though, it was a mess. I'd dumped my school things on the floor and let my clothes just drop when I undressed. On top of everything sprawled my old cloth doll with the two faces. The little book attached to her arm explained her two sides in this way:

> There was a little girl who had a little curl
> Right in the middle of her forehead.
> When she was good, she was very, very good.
> And when she was bad she was horrid.

I hated her "horrid" face and always kept it turned toward the wall, but this morning that side lay face up. She glared at me as if defending her clenched fists, unbuckled shoes, and torn dress. She looked as if she could have said all the nasty things I'd heard in my dream. I put her back in her usual place on the dresser, her smiling side out once again.

# Chapter 3

A few afternoons later, I rescued Ben from a fight on the bus. "I didn't see how it started, Mom, but I think he had a fight at lunch because I saw the playground monitor take Ben, who had a bloody nose, to the nurse. Then on the bus home there was a lot of noise and I saw Ben on the floor."

Looking concerned, my mother examined the black and blue mark under Ben's left eye. He turned away, and his eyes filled with tears; Mom motioned for me to leave. Through the family room door I heard him then, sobbing out his whole rotten day. Mom comforted him.

I wished I were in her arms being soothed, too. After seeing Ben come in from the playground, I worried about him all afternoon and did four of my five word problems wrong. When Ginny corrected my paper, she wrote "20%" at the top as small as possible, knowing how I would feel when I saw the mark.

I'd seen a lot more on the bus than Mom had given me time to tell her. In my mind I replayed the entire scene, beginning with Ben's hat flying over my head.

"Give it back," Ben yelled, starting to go after it.

"Stay in your seat till the bus stops," the driver commanded.

As Ben headed back to his seat, Mike Henry, the biggest boy in third grade, put his foot out and tripped my brother. "You belong up front, Clark, just like in school, so Mrs. Lewis can watch you all the time. Here, take your backpack with you." The backpack landed with a thud on top of Ben, who was now sitting on the floor in a heap.

*Why does Mike have to be so cruel? It's bad enough having to sit in the front of the class without being teased for it.* "Ben, why don't you come sit with me," I called coaxingly.

Melissa, sitting next to the window, objected loudly, "Emily, we'll be squished. There's already three of us in the seat."

I looked pleadingly at Ginny, desperate to get Ben out of there before something worse happened. "I can sit on your lap, Melissa," she offered. "They'll get off in just a few more stops." The dark-haired girl sighed grudgingly as Ginny climbed on top of her.

Ben came without further urging. I felt myself being angry along with him. Melissa complained the whole time that she was being crushed.

Now, as I listened around the corner of the downstairs hall, Ben told Mom how the fight started at noon. Winter weather had returned, and Ben had bunched some wet snow into a hard, heavy ball to lob at Mike Henry. Usually my brother had terrible aim, but today his snowball found its mark — or so it seemed.

"I *wasn't* aiming for his eye!" Ben wailed to Mom. "Honest! It just happened." He sniffled.

Mike had retaliated by tossing one at Ben's eye and, when my brother paused to nurse it, threw snow down his neck.

That evening Mom and Dad sat down to talk in the living room below me while I was upstairs studying for my states test. Later, I was sorry I had strained so hard to listen through the grate.

"The principal tried to call me this afternoon, but I was at a meeting," Mom told Dad. "She asked for our permission to refer Ben to the Child Study Team for psychological testing for his..." Just then the furnace came on, muffling her voice. *Testing? For what? What does he have?* I waited desperately till I could hear again, hoping for at least another clue.

When the blower turned off, it sounded like Dad was reading aloud.

"...Can't sit still, talks too much or interrupts, acts without thinking, doesn't complete tasks, gets bored easily...." *That sure sounds like Ben. Mom thinks he'll have to take strong drugs, so it must be something pretty bad.* Filled with dread of this nameless illness, I bent my ear over the grate to listen more closely, but Mom and Dad must have moved off into the kitchen because their voices were only a soft hum now.

# I'm Somebody Too

The next morning I examined Ben carefully for signs of sickness, but to me he looked just like any other healthy kid finishing his second bowl of cereal. I wondered sadly how he had gotten whatever he had and how long it would be before he'd have to go to the hospital.

Then I almost choked on my cereal. *Is it contagious? Maybe I'll get it, too. Can I take medicine to keep from getting it? I have to find out...but how? Maybe if I tell the school nurse what medicine they're going to give Ben, she can at least tell me what he has. I'll go see her at recess.*

Usually I don't have any problem keeping my mind on my schoolwork, but that morning all I could think about was Ben being taken away, and then me. Would the hospital smell the same as the nursing home where we sang Christmas carols? Would our parents come to see us? Would they get it too? Maybe we'd all die!

I came back to reality with a sickening jolt as Mr. Miller said, "Clear your desk for the spelling test." Spelling test! I had forgotten to study last night. In fact, come to think of it, I hadn't done any homework!

Good thing Ginny corrected that paper too, because I would have been too embarrassed to have anyone else see it. I got 65%. Later that afternoon, when Mr. Miller was recording our grades, he called me to his desk. I concentrated on his bald spot to keep from looking into his friendly blue eyes. It always surprised me that such a young face should go with a bald head. "Emily, yesterday you got a poor mark in math and today, this sixty-five in spelling. What's up with you? Something wrong at home?"

I stood there miserably, not wanting to tell him about my brother's illness. I shrugged. "Nothing," I replied quietly. "I'll do better tomorrow."

"I hope so, Emily, because you're usually such a good student. If you need extra help, just let me know."

Lunchtime — finally. Now I could ask the nurse about Ben's disease. "I have to deliver a message for my mother," I told Ginny hastily, not even giving her a chance to ask if she could come along. I hurried down the corridor to the nurse's office, my heart pounding. *Prepare yourself for the worst kind of news,* I told myself, *then if it's not so bad you'll be relieved.* At least I would get my questions answered.

The nurse's office was right at the end of the next hallway. *When I round the next corner,* I told myself, *I'll see her sitting at her desk. And then I'll find out. For better or for worse, I'll know.*

The office door was closed, and a small sign hung from the doorknob. "At lunch till 12:30. In case of emergency, go to the main office," it read. *Emergency?* I said to myself. *No, this isn't an emergency — yet.* I walked slowly to the cafeteria, hardly hungry.

Mom looked tired when Dad got home from his job at the printing plant. He gathered Mom into his long arms and they stood like that for a long time, saying nothing. After giving them a few seconds to themselves, I walked up close.

"Hi, Dad," I said softly, putting my arms around them both. I breathed in the good smell of his leather jacket.

Letting go of Mom, he bent down to kiss me. His sandy-colored beard, touched with gray, tickled when it brushed my cheek. "How's my other girl?" he said warmly.

Thinking wistfully of all the "horsey-back" rides he'd given me and how he used to balance me on his hands when I was smaller, I asked, "Can we play cards tonight?"

He paused, shooting Mom a look. She frowned and shook her head. "You're already late, and we have so much to do..."

Dad replied, "I don't know yet, Emily. Your mom and I have some things to discuss. But it does sound like fun." He patted me on the back.

Every time I turned around that evening, they were standing near each other, talking quietly. *Probably about Ben*, I thought. *I wish they'd tell me what was going on, too.* Their togetherness made me feel very alone. Ben spent the evening in front of the TV, and I finally went up to my room. Obviously no one wanted to spend time with me that night.

Just before bed, I remembered the math test and the spelling test, and went down to the kitchen. Mom was talking quietly to Dad, but when she saw me, she broke off.

"Emily, are you still up?" Dad said, surprised.

"It's only quarter of nine, Dad," I replied, "and I have to get you to sign this math paper from yesterday. And today's spelling test." I held them out stiffly, watching his face.

His eyebrows shot up, then his usual pleasant expression returned. "Honey, this isn't like you," he said sympathetically, scrawling his name at the top. He held the papers up for Mom to see.

Looking concerned, she put her hand on my forehead. "What happened, Emily? Don't you feel well?"

I shook my head and took a deep breath. *Now or never*, I told myself, trying to swallow the lump in my throat. "I was worried about Ben," I said quietly, afraid to say it out loud.

Mom looked at me quizzically, then glanced at Dad. Cautiously she said, "You mean about the fight he had yesterday, honey? It'll be all right."

"No, not that, Mom," I said. "I'm talking about his illness. What's wrong with him? How did he get it? Will he be all right?"

"Ben's not sick, Emily," Mom denied flatly. "He just got a black eye. He'll be fine." She busied herself with the belt buckle on her pants as if she didn't want to look at me. I stood there awkwardly, not knowing how to break through her silence, waiting for her to say something more.

# I'm Somebody Too

"Now go to bed, okay?" she said, standing up and kissing me on the cheek. "You're my sweetheart," she said, guiding me toward the door and closing it quietly behind me.

They had each other. But I was alone. Why wouldn't anyone talk to me?

# Chapter 4

What a relief not having social studies homework. Today we'd taken our states test, and for the first time in two weeks I didn't have to study for it. Maybe there was something good on TV.

I sank down on the couch in the family room next to my grandfather, who had come with Grandma to watch us while Mom and Dad went to a meeting. He sat in the same place Dad always did. "Would you prefer a nature show, a rerun of *Star Trek,* or basketball?" he asked me.

"The nature show, I guess," I said, disappointed there was nothing good to watch. Besides, as much as I loved my white-haired grandparents, I felt resentful that Grandma and Grandpa were here tonight.

"Mom, I'm almost twelve years old now," I had protested this afternoon when she told me my grandparents were coming. "I don't need a babysitter."

"I know, honey, but Ben does," Mom had replied.

Over the low wall that separated the family room from the kitchen, I could see Grandma settling down to help Ben with his times tables, as Mom had asked.

Suddenly I was glad she had come: I never got anywhere when I tried to review with him.

"What's four times eight, Ben?" Grandma began pleasantly.

"Thirty-six. No, thirty-two," he replied, rocking his chair back and forth, bumping as he went.

"Good. Six times seven."

"Sixty-seven," he said, turning around to see the TV in the family room. The nature show was over and now the music from *Dinosaur Dynasty* started.

What a dumb show. Of course, it was Ben's favorite — anything to do with dinosaurs, he loved. He had a poster of an apatosaurus in his room and a dinosaur wallet (well, he used to have one — he'd lost it on the bus), and, whenever he had some allowance saved, he'd buy dinosaur jellies.

As Patty the apatosaurus was talking to her husband, Stan, Ben strained to catch the words from his place in the next room.

"Six times seven," Grandma persisted, still calm. My gratitude and admiration for the soft, white-haired woman doubled. I would have lost my temper with Ben as soon as he started to watch TV.

Silence. More firmly this time, Grandma said, "Ben, you have a test tomorrow. If you want help on your times tables, you'll need to pay attention."

Paying attention — Mom and Dad had talked to us about that a lot lately. Mom said the school had tested Ben, and he has "attention problems, or ADD," spelling the letters out one by one. She said that's why he forgets everything and never sits still.

I was really surprised when Dad said that Ben is very smart. *Then how come I always get As and Bs on my report card, and he gets Bs and Cs?* I didn't say that out loud, but Dad must've guessed what I was thinking, because he said, "Some people with ADD have difficulty in school because they have trouble paying attention long enough for them to learn." Turning to Ben, he continued, "Once you learn how to concentrate more, you'll do much better."

My brother said nothing, just kind of kept his chin down and looked up at Dad through his uncombed hair. I could tell he didn't believe Dad, either.

From my spot in the family room, I could see Grandma struggling to be patient.

"Six times seven is forty-two, remember? Say it after me," Grandma instructed.

"*I know*, Grandma," Ben replied grudgingly, bumping his chair again.

"Four times eight."

"Thirty-one. No, thirty-two."

"Right. Seven times eight."

"Twenty-four. No, fifty-six."

"Good. Now. Six times seven."

"Forty-eight." *Ben still hadn't learned six times seven,* I thought, *and no wonder — his eyes are fixed on the TV again. Poor Grandma — she might as well be talking to a wall.* I got off the couch and went into the kitchen to see if I could help.

"Ben, when you can't remember times tables, you should write them down ten times," I suggested. "That's how I learned the states for my test."

By now, however, my brother was completely caught up in Stan's invention of a new dinosaur egg-warmer to free Patty from sitting on hatchlings for so long. Ben got up and drifted into the family room to his favorite chair in front of the TV.

*He may be brilliant,* I thought angrily, *but what good is that if he can't learn his times tables?* I was also embarrassed at the way he'd treated Grandma. She was just trying to help.

"I hope you fail your test," I said under my breath. Then I put my hand over my mouth, ashamed. How could I be angry at someone who had ADD?

As Grandma sighed and closed the math book, Grandpa came into the kitchen and said in a hushed tone, "Want me to try for awhile?"

"No, I don't think it will do any good," she whispered sadly. "He just doesn't have the attention span."

Personally, I couldn't see how watching TV instead of doing homework had anything to do with paying attention. After all, when Dad helped Ben do something fun like putting together his rocket, he could sit there for hours asking questions and gluing things. And then for just as long afterward, he would tell you everything about it—even though you couldn't care less. But when it came to something boring like

times tables, suddenly Ben couldn't pay attention —
or maybe he didn't want to.

Still, both my grandparents *and* my parents acted
sad instead of mad. There must be something more to
this than I was seeing. What were they all hiding?

I'm Somebody Too

# Chapter 5

The next afternoon the sun shone and I managed to forget all the trouble with Ben for a few hours. It was the perfect day to share my newest discovery with Ginny — the horse farm. For the first day in a long time I had my best friend all to myself, because Melissa had a dentist appointment.

Standing with my arms on the high fence, I watched a horse race to the edge of the field. Through the bare trees I could see the pink glow of the sky on the horizon. Ginny's pale face looked rosy in the February sunset, and the way her wispy, light hair was blowing reminded me of when we used to swing for hours in a patch of sunlight in the backyard.

Ginny was always complaining that her hair was too slippery to hold a ponytail, so mostly she just pulled it back with barrettes and let it hang. That's how she'd worn it in the picture Mom had taken of us starting kindergarten together. In first grade we had both worn pigtails with matching bows and lost our first tooth the same week. Her pigtails always came out after recess, but I helped her redo them.

# I'm Somebody Too

Ginny cared a lot more about how she looked than I did; I combed my hair because Mom was always telling me to keep it out of my eyes or she'd cut it short. But then I wouldn't look like Ginny.

Not that I did, anyway. She was small and light; I was taller and more solid. In summer my long muscles gleamed through my tan legs, and hers looked more rounded, and pale like her hair. She complained that she never got a good tan until August and always admired mine, which came the first day we sat out in May and stayed with me all summer. Her mother was always telling her to put on sunscreen so she wouldn't burn, but I never had to worry.

Everything I had ever wanted or enjoyed was wrapped up with Ginny. We got the same baby dolls with stars in their hair when we were little. We'd learned to ride bikes the same summer, divided the fruit in my lunch and the cookies in hers, and camped out in the backyard together. From first grade through fourth, we had called each other at seven o'clock every evening, but this year she started taking organ lessons after dinner, and other times her line was busy.

I felt privileged to show her the horses and was glad that Melissa hadn't come along.

Ginny looked at her watch. "It's almost five o'clock. I've got to go home."

We rode our bikes side by side in the wide field toward the road. "Let's pretend that our bikes are horses," I said. "Mine's Black Beauty. What's yours?"

# I'm Somebody Too

"I don't know any horses' names," she replied.

Neither did I, really, but hers had to have a name. "How about National Velvet?" I suggested. "I think I once heard of a horse by that name."

"Okay," she said.

"Come on, Velvet, I'll race you." I took off and was soon far ahead. As the breeze slid past my cheeks, I imagined that I was racing Black Beauty along a white sandy beach. My legs pumped like those of the powerful horse I imagined beneath me, and we bolted across the sand for the joy of it.

Then I noticed how far behind me Ginny had fallen. "I'm freezing," she said when she caught up with me. Guiltily I noticed how red her nose was; I guess she wasn't enjoying this as much as I was.

"Here, take my scarf. It isn't too much farther now." I stayed with Ginny the rest of the way home, even though I wanted to sail with the wind.

# Chapter 6

One morning later that week, Mom woke us up fifteen minutes early. "I'm going to drive you to school this morning, so please get up now," she told Ben and me.

"Why?" I said, touching my feet gingerly to the cold hardwood floor, then reaching for my slippers.

"Because I have a meeting at school," she replied.

I thought guiltily about the math and spelling tests. "With Mr. Miller?" I asked. Actually, I realized suddenly, maybe it would be a relief. She could tell him I was failing my tests because our family was upset about my brother and then maybe somebody would tell me what was really going on.

"No, with Mrs. Lewis."

"Oh." *That makes sense, I guess, since Ben's the one with the disease.* Still, I felt disappointed. Sighing, I thought *I'll just have to manage by myself as I've been doing all along. Mom and Dad have enough to do with Ben; they don't need my problems too.*

Through my eyelet curtains, I peered out at the beautiful sunrise. Yesterday's wind had died. Since Mom was driving us to school, I wouldn't have to dress

# I'm Somebody Too

like an Eskimo to keep warm on the long bus ride, as I usually did.

Lately it seemed I had nothing to wear. Oh, there were plenty of winter things — even a black velvet vest that I loved — but I was tired of all of them and longed for short sleeves and bare arms. However, spring was still many weeks away.

Rummaging through my drawer, I found a plain pair of blue pants that I'd forgotten about. And here was a pink turtleneck with blue cats on it. Too bad they weren't horses instead. Ginny often wore blue tops to match her eyes, but mine were brown, so it didn't matter. I decided to braid my hair like the old-fashioned girl in the book I'd read the other day, and was quite satisfied when I was done. All I needed was some bows to decorate the two ends. *There.* I checked again in the mirror. *Perfect.*

Except for the sweatshirt. *Old-fashioned girls don't wear sweatshirts,* I reasoned; *they wear blouses. That plain white one that Mom bought me to go with my jumper will do just fine. Yes, it's perfect with the braids, but the plain blue pants looked boring now.* I changed into dark pink corduroy ones with little purple flowers on them, and then pulled on white socks and my good shoes. *An old-fashioned girl would never wear sneakers. Besides, they make my feet look even bigger than they are.*

I couldn't wait to show Ginny. Maybe she would dress like an old-fashioned girl tomorrow. I would offer to rebraid her hair at noon if it fell out, I thought generously.

"Emily, you look picture-perfect this morning," Mom said, kissing me on the temple. "Here's your vitamin."

"Do I look like an old-fashioned girl?" I asked, wanting to hear more.

"You certainly do. Especially the braids." Her gaze traveled down to my feet. "Umm, about the shoes..."

"Oh, Mom, please! I just can't wear sneakers — it would spoil everything. I'll be careful." She nodded understandingly and smiled. "I'm sure you will."

"Now Ben," I heard her say as I walked into the pantry to get my cereal. "You've worn that shirt four days in a row and it's dirty. Can you please go change?" Sighing loudly, he stamped upstairs.

I carried my cereal to the big wooden table in the eating area and pulled up a bench. This was one of my favorite parts of the house since Mom and Dad had it remodeled last summer. They took out the wall with the little window and made the room five feet longer; now we had big windows all around, and a door to the backyard. The new dark woodwork matched the table and benches, and a large oak door closed off the whole kitchen from the hallway.

The bundle of wheat hanging in a basket from the wall matched the design on the wallpaper, tan and green on a white background. As we drove to school that morning, I saw those colors again in the fields of snow with only evergreens and dry grasses for color.

For a long time I had avoided telling Mom about going to the horse farm. She might not like my riding so far out in the country. "I wonder what it's like to ride bikes if you turn the other way off Watson Road," I said casually.

"Kind of hilly," she replied, keeping her eyes on the road. "Remember, we went that way to get our Christmas tree last year."

"I bet there's a good view from up on the hill," I continued.

"Yes, there probably is. Be careful to wear your helmet and stay well off the road, though. Cars go fast on that road."

*Oh, good!* I thought. *She didn't tell me not to go.* "Okay," I agreed happily.

"Can I go too?" Ben asked eagerly. *No!* I cried silently. *He'll spoil everything if he comes along. I'd have to watch that he doesn't get run over, and he would probably talk too much.*

To my relief, Mom didn't even pause to consider his request. "No, you're too young." *Whew!*

When I got to my classroom, only Mr. Miller and Mary Saunders were there. I hardly gave the plain-looking girl a second glance, since I didn't know her very well. Laying my books on my desk, I thought about Ginny wondering why I wasn't at the bus stop. She'd be worried that I was sick.

Mary came over to my desk. "How come you're so early this morning, Emily?"

As I was telling her about Mom's driving me, I noticed that she was wearing a tiny gold horse on her necklace. "I like your horse. Where'd you get it?"

"My mom gave it to me when I started to take riding lessons."

"Where do you take them? How long have you done it?" The questions tumbled out of my mouth almost before I realized it.

"Over at Hillyard's," she replied. "I started a few weeks after Christmas."

"Where's Hillyard's?"

"It's the big pink barn on Harris Road. It's so far back you hardly notice it, but the fences for the horses come right out to the road."

"Oh, *that* place," I said, recognizing her description of the farm where Ginny and I watched the horses. "I've been there."

Mary looked down at her necklace and then brushed her fine brown bangs out of her eyes with a gesture that reminded me of Mom. "Do you ride, too?"

"No," I replied. "But I wish I did. Do you like it?"

"It's fun. This winter we've stayed inside, where we're protected from the wind, but in the spring we'll get to go outside. They even have trails through the woods. That's what I really want to do." She smiled shyly. "Maybe you could sign up for a trail ride someday."

"Oh, but you must be such a good rider, and I don't know anything! You'd be bored going at my speed."

"No, I think it would be fun," she said happily.

Kids from my bus started pouring into the room, and I saw Ginny in the hall talking to someone. *That blue jacket looks familiar,* I thought, *but it couldn't be because the hair is too short. Short, curly hair the same dark color as....It's Melissa! She's cut her hair!*

A group of girls flocked around Melissa, touching her soft curls. My own hair, compressed into a braid, bristled against my neck like a bottle brush.

Ginny plunked her backpack on her desk next to mine and said excitedly, "Melissa got her hair cut, and it looks so cute. How do you think I'd look with short hair?" *So much for looking like matching old-fashioned girls,* I thought.

Eyeing her, I replied truthfully, "Your hair would probably lie flat against your head. Melissa's is very full and curly, so it bounces."

Ginny's face fell as if I'd slapped her. She sat down without saying anything more and busied herself with the work on the board.

The rest of the day at school, Ginny avoided me, obviously still hurt by my comment about her hair. When it was time to correct each other's math papers, she traded with the girl across the aisle from her instead of me. I pretended that I had to finish work at lunch so I wouldn't have to see her with Melissa, and I made sure I was the last one on the bus so the seat next to Ginny would be full. It had been a long day, and I decided to apologize even though I hadn't said anything mean on purpose.

That evening at seven o'clock I waited for Ginny to call me, but the phone remained silent. When I finally called her house at seven-thirty, her father said she wasn't home. As I sat on the steps feeling lonely, Dad followed Ben up to his room and closed the door. Then Mom turned out the kitchen light and headed up the stairs, looking startled when she met me sitting there.

I could always tell what Mom was interested in by reading the titles of the books she carried around. She seldom drove the car or waited for anything without a book to keep her busy. She had often read to us in restaurants and on long trips, and I had picked up the habit, too.

Tonight she had not one but three books, all on paying attention. "Are you planning to read all those tonight, Mom?" I asked, my hand on the heavy oak banister.

She laughed, that short, coughing sound that had no humor in it. "Till I fall asleep," she said, mounting the stairs. She already looked tired; still, it wouldn't surprise me if she finished them all. She could finish a whole novel in two nights if she really liked it.

From behind Ben's door I heard Dad and Ben singing a familiar tune over and over. But the sound seemed a million miles away, and my world remained silent and lonely; I didn't know what to do with myself. I made a cup of peppermint tea for Mom and took it to her room. She looked up, surprised. "Oh, Emily, thank you. How thoughtful." She put the cup on her nightstand and resumed her reading, but I interrupted again. "Ginny didn't call tonight."

"She's probably shopping or something," she replied absently, her eyes on the book. *Look at me!* I cried silently. *I'm losing my best friend and you don't even care.*

Leaving her room quietly, I thought of what I could do to make this lonely evening pass. *Homework: done. TV: nothing good on. Games? No one to play with.* I ignored the voice inside that kept repeating, *Ginny doesn't want to talk to you.* Finally I decided to lose myself in a book like Mom does, and went to look for one.

Loosening my braids, I felt my scalp relax. A few minutes later, I was so deep into my novel that I didn't even notice that no one kissed me goodnight. But the next morning, when I woke still fully dressed with the book lying beside me, I felt like nobody's child. They hadn't even bothered to tuck me in.

# Chapter 7

Two hours later, when I got to the bus stop, Ginny looked strange, though at first I couldn't figure out why. She smiled at me as if she'd forgotten yesterday. "I got my hair cut," she said excitedly. "Look!"

She pulled her hat off by the pom-pom and I stared. Her hair was cut around her ears and her bangs were razored in uneven layers. "My sister says I look at least fourteen," she said proudly.

"It's...it's nice," I said, because I knew she was waiting for a comment. "You sure look different." Taking it as a compliment, she nodded confidently and replaced her hat.

Ginny repeated the same demonstration when Melissa took her place in the bus line. I didn't stick around at school to see if other girls liked it better than I did.

As soon as recess began, Mary Saunders was beside me. "What are you doing after school today?" she asked.

"Um, nothing," I replied absently, putting my papers in my desk. I wondered glumly how I was going to get through lunch with Melissa and Ginny gloating about their hair.

"Oops, I forgot. You have chorus, don't you?" Out of the corner of my eye, I saw Ginny grab her coat and slip out the door without looking back.

In that instant I decided to quit chorus. "No, I'm not going back there again," I murmured, almost to myself. Ginny was the only reason I'd joined, and somehow I didn't think she'd notice anymore whether I was there or not.

"What did you say?" Mary asked, tucking her straight, shiny hair behind her ears.

More loudly this time, I repeated, "I'm quitting. How did you know I took chorus, anyway?"

"Oh, I always see you going downstairs with Ginny when my mom comes to get me," she replied casually. She walked me over to the coat rack.

"I thought you took the bus," I said, puzzled.

"Not on Wednesdays, when I ride. I have to go right home to change, and then she takes me to the stable for my lesson. I was thinking maybe you could come watch today if you weren't busy. That is, if you want to," she finished uncertainly. She looked around. "Where's Ginny?" she asked.

"I don't know," I replied, trying to sound as if it didn't matter. "I guess she had something else to do." We walked out the door and down the hall to the cafeteria. That was the first day I could ever remember not having lunch with my best friend, except when one of us was sick. At first the strangeness of it made my food seem tasteless and hard to swallow, but for Mary's sake I pretended everything was okay.

"So do you want to come and watch me ride this afternoon?" she asked.

"Yes!" I said without hesitation. "Will the people at the stable mind?"

Taking a bite of her fluffernutter sandwich, she shook her head. "People always watch," she replied. "You can sit up in the observation deck where the little brothers and sisters wait, or you can just stand around below, near the ring. If you stay below, I'll let you pet my horse and help me walk it out of the stall. I usually ride Monroe."

As we lined up to go outside, Ben's class passed us. He came over to me quickly and said hurriedly, "Do you have any money I can borrow for milk? I lost mine." I gave him my last twenty-five cents and he ran to join his class in the cafeteria line.

"That's my brother," I explained.

"What grade is he in?" asked Mary.

"Third."

"Mine's in fourth. Aren't brothers a pain?"

My eyes traveled to the lunch line, where Ben was throwing a quarter up in the air and catching it. He must've missed, because he dropped to his knees and started searching. When the girl behind Ben started to move ahead and get food, she stumbled over his ankle, breaking her milk carton on the floor. The lunch lady spoke sharply to him, and after a few moments he got out of line and shuffled over to a table without talking to anyone.

"Yeah, especially when they have a deadly disease," I murmured to myself. *Poor Ben. He doesn't have anything to drink or anyone to eat with.* I sighed, wishing I could do something to help.

Mary turned to me, startled. "What did you say?"

I looked at my feet to avoid my confusion. *Did I really let that slip out? No one is supposed to know — not even me.* I coughed and pretended I hadn't heard her, searching desperately for a way to talk myself out of this. Our class line was moving outside for recess, giving me a few extra minutes to think. But it didn't do any good.

Stepping through the door to the playground, Mary turned to me again. The sunlight brought out reddish tones in her brown hair. "Did you say your brother has a deadly disease? What is it?" she asked quietly.

Suddenly I realized why I hadn't told Ginny: I no longer trusted her enough to keep a secret. But I felt reassured by the kindness in Mary's eyes and the way she was keeping her voice down.

"No. Yes. Well, I'm not sure," I replied, sighing. "My parents told us he has trouble paying attention. But I think it's more than that because they look real sad and don't want to talk about it. So it must be something pretty bad."

# I'm Somebody Too

"How do you know about this if they don't want to talk about it?"

"I hear them whispering a lot and Ben had to go to the doctor a couple times. Promise you won't tell," I continued, and told her what I'd heard by listening through the grate.

We were walking around on the parking lot because the ground was muddy between patches of melting snow. I didn't want to get my boots dirty. "Does your brother take medicine or anything?" asked Mary.

"Not that I know of. But they were talking about it. Mom said she didn't want to give him anything that would make him act like a zombie." I laughed ruefully. "He's already so out of it, he can barely make it through the lunch line."

Mary pulled a candy bar out of her pocket and started opening it. "Want some?" she asked.

"Sure. Your lunch looked good today," I added, glad to talk about something else. "My mom always makes me pack *healthy* stuff like carrots or fruit, with baloney or tuna sandwiches."

She laughed. "My mom gets on those kicks sometimes, too. I was lucky today." She gave me half. It tasted better than anything had in days.

From the other side of the parking lot came loud chanting. "Wonder what's going on over there?" I said.

"I think it's cheerleading. Sandy Stone's older sister cheers for the high school boys' basketball team.

Sandy must be teaching some cheers." Eight or nine girls had gathered around to watch Sandy and her friend Jessica demonstrate a jump. Melissa and Ginny drifted over and hung around the edge of the crowd.

"Do you like basketball?" I asked Mary.

"It's okay to play, but I don't like cheerleading. I think girls do it just to impress boys." She must have seen Ginny at that moment because she stopped suddenly and looked at me, embarrassed. "Of course, not everyone's that way. I guess some girls just enjoy it the way I enjoy horseback riding. If you want to go over, I'll talk to you later."

She thinks Ginny's still my best friend, I realized. "No, that's okay. I don't like it either." Turning our backs to the voices of the shouting girls, we walked the other way across the pavement. Inside my heavy mittens my hands felt a little sweaty, and I pulled them off, grateful for the sun. Then I removed my hat, and my hair fell around my face.

"Are you going to get *your* hair cut?" Mary asked, a teasing smile on her face.

"No, I like mine long. Ginny looks like she's trying to be older." Mary smiled as if she understood exactly how I felt about my friendship with Ginny.

"Good. When you learn to ride, you'll look nice with a ponytail hanging down from under your hard hat." She smiled merrily and ran a few steps. "This is a trot." I caught up with her. "And this is a canter. Catch me if you can."

# *Chapter 8*

Mom almost didn't let me ride my bike to the stable that afternoon. "You can't ride your bike in the snow, Emily. When it's slushy like this, you could fall."

"But Mom, it's eighty degrees out!"

She looked out the kitchen window and seemed surprised. "Yes, I guess you're right. It has warmed up." *Geez,* I thought, *doesn't she even notice the warm sunshine today? She had to walk in it to get to her car after work. But then, she always seems to be thinking of something else lately. I guess she's feeling pretty bad about Ben.*

For a moment she looked at me as if she really saw me. Her eyes twinkled. "It's not eighty — more like thirty-five — but after the last few weeks of bad weather, I guess it must feel like eighty to you. Okay. You may ride your bike — but stay out of the mud."

She didn't ask where I was going, and I was glad. Somehow I didn't want her to know about the horses, because I was afraid she wouldn't approve.

"Are you going with Ginny?" she asked, spraying the window over the sink with glass cleaner and starting to rub it with a paper towel.

How I wanted to stay and tell her all about Ginny! But I couldn't resist the golden afternoon and the promise of watching a horseback-riding lesson. "I'm not sure. She may be busy," I replied, pulling on my boots. "See you later."

"Come back before dark," she called as I went out the door.

*Spring can't be far off now. When winter has left for good, I'll ride my bike every day to the stable and watch the horses.* Bringing my ten-speed to a stop at the bottom of the hill, I listened gratefully to the trickle of the melting snow running down the gutter into the sewer. The little stream sparkled in the sun.

"Go in the people door, and you'll see a big ring. I'll watch for you," Mary had said when I asked her where to meet her. Stepping inside, I almost ran into a curving wall as high as my chin that separated the large ring from the area where the horses were kept. A wide aisle ran the length of the barn, with horses looking inquiringly out of stalls on either side.

Mary emerged from a room at the end of the hall, wearing tall boots and a black hard hat. "Hi, Emily. Come on, I'll show you how to tack him up."

I was surprised to find the faint smell of manure inoffensive, almost pleasant. Nevertheless, I glanced cautiously at the straw-strewn floor before setting another foot on it. "Mom will never forgive me if I come home with poopy boots," I giggled.

"Don't worry, it's kept pretty clean," Mary said reassuringly. Leading me into the second stall, she said, "This is Monroe. He's nice to ride, but gets a little grumpy when we tighten his girth. You can pet him."

I eyed the grayish white animal curiously. I had never been this close to a horse before, unless you count the ones that mounted police use to patrol the parks in the summer. Somehow, now that I was thinking about riding a horse myself, it looked bigger. Carefully, I reached out and touched Monroe's long, flat flank. The fur, or hair, I guess you call it, was short and coarse—not at all what I expected. I could feel the muscles underneath. As the horse shifted its feet in the narrow, dark stall, I backed away.

"Come on, Monroe," Mary beckoned, slipping a bridle over the animal's head and pulling gently on the reins. After adjusting the stirrups, she tightened a band under his belly. The horse shifted his feet and wagged his head slightly. "Now, Monroe, it's okay. Don't be so grumpy." Her tone reassured me. If that was grumpy behavior for a horse, I had little to fear.

"The only thing you really have to watch out for is the feet," she instructed. "Just be sure that you don't stand right behind him, or he might step on you by accident. If you're behind his back feet and you startle him, he might kick. Horses don't like to be surprised from behind." I nodded, etching every word into my memory. I wanted to avoid accidents at all costs.

Mary led Monroe toward the ring, where four

other girls were mounting horses. Each wore a hard hat and boots; one had on white pants and a fitted red jacket like I'd seen in the movies. They all looked so tall up there, and so sure of themselves.

The riders walked their horses around the edge of the ring for several minutes. *That doesn't look too hard,* I thought. But then, as Nanette, the instructor, stood in the middle and issued commands to each girl in turn, my respect for their skill increased a hundred times. One minute Monroe plodded placidly, the next he was loping along and Mary was bobbing up and down in perfect rhythm with his stride. Looking more closely, I noticed that she was apparently holding on with only the reins.

"Good, Mary. Keep your heels down. Look straight ahead. Nice posting. Now let him walk," Nanette called. Almost immediately the horse and rider slowed and resumed plodding around the ring. Mary leaned forward and patted Monroe on the neck.

*Now how did Mary do that?* As I listened during the next hour, I realized it was some combination of keeping your heels down and squeezing with your legs. This certainly would be more interesting than singing alto in the chorus. I envisioned myself sitting astride the horse with the horse running — cantering? trotting? I wasn't sure what the right word was — down a tree-lined path in the fall. And right behind me would be...Mary.

I realized with a start that I hadn't thought about

Ginny for a whole hour, hadn't even missed her. Looking at my watch, I judged that chorus was over and she was taking the late bus home with Melissa. They were probably practicing today's music or one of those dumb cheers they'd learned at recess. In a way it was a relief not to be tagging along, feeling like an outsider.

Mary smiled at me as she rode past. Here was a place where I was wanted, where I could belong on my own terms, not on Ginny's.

# Chapter 9

A couple of days later I brought home a math test with a big, fat "100%" on top. I thought I had the only perfect paper in the class, and I couldn't wait to show it to Mom — especially after the bad ones I'd brought home earlier. Even though I was still worried about Ben, somehow it was easier because of having Mary as my friend.

Today I was the first one hurrying up the hill to our house, with Ben trailing behind by about thirty feet. *The ache in my throat seems to have gone away,* I noticed suddenly. Maybe it was the sunshine that was making me feel better — three whole days of hatless, loose-coated weather in February. Or maybe it was because I was getting to know Mary and learn about riding. She lived just a few streets away, and Mom had let me take my bike there yesterday. We had ridden all around her neighborhood, pretending we were thoroughbreds. She showed me a book about wild horses on an island called Assateague. I would have to look it up on a map.

The only thing that hadn't improved so far was

# I'm Somebody Too

Ben — at least, not that I'd heard of. Yesterday Mom started giving him little yellow pills at breakfast when she gave me my vitamin. I guess she was satisfied that he wouldn't act like a zombie, after all. Maybe they would even make him well.

I had to wait while Mom unlocked the front door; by the time she came, Ben was right behind me. He stepped over my backpack as I laid it on the rug in the hall, knocking it over and dropping his jacket beside it in his rush for the bathroom. I slipped off my shoes and hung my coat in the closet.

Mom returned to the kitchen; through the open door I saw her pick up the phone that had been lying on the counter. "I have to go, Mamie." That's what she called Grandma, who was Dad's mom. Then she added quietly, "The kids are home." A pause. "Okay, I'll try that. Thanks for listening."

Mom stepped into the hallway and immediately picked up her stockinged foot. She held it out with as much distaste as a cat with a wet paw. "Ben, please wipe up this water. But first take off your wet shoes."

She went to the kitchen and returned with a paper towel for him. Standing over him while he wiped the floor, she asked, "How did your spelling test go today?"

"What spelling test?" he replied, leaving the wet towel on the floor and starting for the kitchen. As Mom picked it up, she said, "Didn't you have a spelling test?"

# I'm Somebody Too

"Oh, yeah. I forgot." He opened a cupboard.

She leaned on the counter next to him. "Well, how did you do? May I see it? Where's your backpack?" *All this fuss about a spelling test,* I thought. *Why is it so important to her? Didn't she know Ben could never think about anything till he'd had his snack?*

But Mom didn't wait for any more answers from Ben. She rummaged through his backpack herself and finally pulled out a crumpled piece of lined paper from under his lunch bag. "Is this it?" she asked, showing it to him. He nodded briefly, barely looking up from his peanut butter and crackers.

Mom seemed to hold her breath as she surveyed the paper. Then she asked quietly, "Ben, did your teacher do anything different today when you took the test?"

We both watched his throat muscles strain as he swallowed the cracker before answering. "No," he answered. "Like what?"

She took a long breath before replying, "Did she give you extra time or repeat the words for you? Or let you take the test in a special place?"

Ben frowned and shook his head. "No, it was just a regular test. Mom, do you think if ...."

I couldn't wait any longer. Since Mom was so interested in tests today, I'd give her something to be really happy about. "Mom, you know that big math test I studied for? Well, look at this!" I smiled triumphantly, handing her the unwrinkled sheet from my folder. She glanced quickly at it and forced a smile. I could tell she was really thinking about something else. "Good job, honey." She looked at the clock and opened the fridge, bending down to reach inside.

"Mom, I think I was the only one in the class who got a hundred," I tried again.

She stood up, holding a dish of leftover meatballs. "You always were a good student." She smiled again and turned to put the dish in the microwave.

I gritted my teeth to hold back the wail that almost escaped me. *That's all you're going to say, after all that studying and getting the only hundred in the class? What will it take to get you to notice me?* I screamed silently at her slim figure, now bent over the cutting board. *If I get bad marks, you don't pay attention. If I get the best in the class, you don't care either! Yet Ben gets a bad mark on a spelling test, just like he always does, and you ask a million questions.*

Mom straightened up and rubbed her temples. *She looks so tired and worried,* I noticed guiltily. *How can I be angry at her?* "Emily, please go up and get me a couple of aspirins for my headache," she asked.

"Sure, Mom," I said willingly. I felt better doing something nice to make up for the mean things I'd just been thinking, even though she had no way of hearing my thoughts.

Later, when I went to my room, the doll with two faces was staring at me, her smile seeming to mock the unspoken anger I held inside.

"Creep," I said, grabbing her off the shelf and throwing her into the deepest corner of my closet. "What do you know about happiness? You don't have to live with a dopey brother and a mother who doesn't care about you. All you ever think about is keeping your clothes pretty, like those dumb cheerleaders Ginny likes!"

I sat down to read, resolving to ignore the bad feelings until they went away and I felt like the nice girl with the pretty curl again — the one everyone was counting on me to be.

But I couldn't keep my thoughts on the book. Instead, I wanted to run away from the voice inside that kept insisting, *Mom only cares about Ben. No one cares about you.*

Running down the stairs, I grabbed my coat and stuck my head in the kitchen. "I'm going for a walk," I said, and ran out the door before Mom could ask me where I was going.

Behind the houses across the street from us lay a huge golf course surrounded by woods and fields. We were never allowed to walk on the course in nice weather because we might get hit by a flying golf ball. But in the last hour the temperature had dropped and it looked like rain again — or maybe snow. No one would play golf on a day like this when the sky was the color of a gray file cabinet and the leftover snow matched. *Even I wouldn't be outside if anyone cared to stop me,* I thought.

# I'm Somebody Too

There were no shadows — rather, everything was the color of shadows. In the gloom a small gray bird sat on a branch, all fluffed out against the gray bark, gray snow, gray sky. *It feels like the sameness and bleakness of our house,* I said to myself. *This must be what it feels like in* The Lion, the Witch, and the Wardrobe — *always winter but never Christmas. The same arguments, the same reminders five million times. The same problems over and over again. Just getting through until the next day, when it feels the same.*

I felt my throat swell and my eyes fill with tears. *I won't cry,* I said fiercely, *I won't.* A long field stretched before me, gentle hills rippling. Zipping my jacket all the way up to my chin, I ran as far as I could. The tears blew back against my temples and stung my face, but I didn't care. When I was cold enough to cancel out the whining voice inside, I headed for home.

# Chapter 10

That evening I thought I'd never get to sleep. Below me, in the living room, my parents settled in for their usual late-evening conversation. Over the years I had learned a lot about my father and his boss at the printing plant as well as about Mom's job at the library. I also had a pretty good idea of my parents' real feelings about our relatives and neighbors, and last year I even got a preview of what we were getting for Christmas. Funny they never realized that I could hear most of what they said.

"You know, after everything we told Ben's teacher about accommodating his ADD, she gave him a standard spelling test again, and he flunked it — as usual!" Mom said. Tonight nature blew and moaned, carrying Dad's low-pitched comments away.

"It would have been so easy to put him in a quieter place to take the test," Mom continued. "There are so many ways she could've helped him — given him a different word list, let him use the computer..." Dad interrupted for a moment, and then she resumed, her voice higher and angrier, "After all the information we've given the school, from the best clinic in town, the teacher doesn't even follow the doctor's suggestions! I guess I'll just have to go in there tomorrow and tell her again."

For the millionth time I struggled to understand this mysterious illness that was to blame for all Ben's problems. *How could giving him different schoolwork make him well again?* I puzzled that question over and over without an answer until I fell asleep.

The voices I heard in my dream frightened me.

In my dream I lay in the darkness with my eyes closed. It seemed that Mom and Dad had company downstairs because many voices spoke softly. Although I couldn't understand them at first, I sensed they were deciding my brother's fate without consulting me. Through my closed eyes I saw my mother's worried eyes darting from one side of the room to the other, listening to an argument and trying to decide what to do. The voices became loud and clear.

"Give him medicine."

"He doesn't need medicine. He's just a brat. There's nothing wrong with him that a good swift kick in the pants won't cure."

"Treat him in a different way and he'll act better."

"Take him to the hospital and maybe he'll get better."

"Send him away. There's no hope for him."

More and more accusers joined the chorus, including the ones I had so often imagined whenever

# I'm Somebody Too

Ben made a fuss in public. An old lady in the grocery store frowned as Ben whined for candy. A mother on the playground accused five-year-old Ben of throwing sand in the eyes of her two-year-old. Ben's teacher and the principal stood by, shaking their heads. Mike Henry's mother joined the throng, condemning Ben for never playing nicely with her son, and pointing out that Mike was already a soccer champion. Ben's coach came by to add that Ben would never amount to anything since he couldn't even play soccer like a regular kid. All the voices blended with the wind in a high-pitched moan.

"No!" cried my mother, covering her ears with her hands. "He's just a little boy. You don't understand — he has a terrible disease and he just can't help it. Please be kind to him."

Then the smiling side of my two-faced doll stepped up to reproach me. *How could you be jealous of Ben? He could be dying, and you're mad because your parents didn't praise you for getting a good mark on one test. How small can you be, Emily? You have to put up with him and try to be his friend — maybe the only friend he's got.* I realized that her smile was no more real than my mother's laugh.

I woke then with my hands over my ears. As I kicked my blankets aside to cool off, I noticed that my sheets were soaked with sweat. A while later I woke again from the same dream, exhausted, cold this time, and aching all over. It went like that all night while unseen forces seemed to argue my brother's fate.

The new day brought little comfort when it finally dawned. Outside my window I could see a dusting of snow on the ground and more of it blowing sideways through the big tree in our backyard. *Those must've been the branches that rubbed against each other all night. No wonder they moaned — they were probably sore.*

As Ben and I trudged to the bus stop against the wind, my nose and throat felt just as raw as the branches. Under the snow, the ground still felt soft from the thaw. As we walked to the bus stop, my ears ached even though I had a hat on. Snow got in the neck of my coat and into my storm cuffs. By the time we reached school, I was really chilled.

Toward the end of science class I received a note from the office to meet Mom at Ben's classroom for a ride home. *Good. I won't have to face the wind again.* Once home, I took a warm shower to clear up the fog of pain that seemed to have collected inside my head, neck, and shoulders.

At five-thirty, when I turned on my bedroom lamp, even my eyes were aching. I clicked off the light and dozed until Dad called me for supper.

"How's my girl tonight?" When he tousled my hair in his usual greeting, even my scalp hurt. "I don't feel too well," I replied. As I said this, I didn't try to straighten my shoulders or even smile like I usually did; I had to convince Mom to let me stay home.

# I'm Somebody Too

"What's the matter, Emily?" she asked.

After I told her how I felt, she said pleasantly, "There are a lot of colds going around. Drink some orange juice and we'll put a vaporizer in your room tonight. You'll probably feel better tomorrow."

I said nothing aloud, but my inner voice continued: *You have to see this time, Mom, that I'm really sick and need to stay home tomorrow. I'm sorry,* I continued silently. *I know you've already taken off several times this week for Ben, but please...*

The next morning even she had to admit that I was sick when the thermometer registered 104 degrees. Suddenly she stopped insisting I would be okay and devoted herself to playing nurse, giving me medicine for my fever, urging me to take a cool bath, and vowing to call Dr. Bernstein as soon as his office opened. I guess she figured if she was going to take a day off for me to be sick, she might as well do everything she could to make me well.

I would have gone to school just to please her if my head didn't ache so much. My throat also seemed to have a mind of its own. The wind outside had finally worn itself out, but I felt as if I'd been screaming for two days straight.

My fever was a little better when the nurse took my temperature, and Mom seemed to relax, busying herself with reading all the magazines in the office. Finally we were shown to one of the small examining rooms.

"Well, what seems to be the problem today?" asked Dr. Bernstein when he came in.

Mom spoke for me like she usually did. "Emily has a sore throat and a fever," she replied. *A sore throat doesn't nearly begin to describe it,* I thought. *Why doesn't she let me talk for myself?*

"And," she added, "I wanted to ask you questions about Ben's Ritalin."

The pediatrician's pale blue eyes shifted calmly from Mom to me and back again. "I'd like to have a look at Emily first," he replied. "How about if you wait in the other room while I examine her?"

It hurt when I swallowed nervously. *Will I have to take off my clothes? I hate that. On the other hand, now is my big chance to ask him about Ben.* I took a deep breath and waited.

Fortunately, he didn't ask me to undress, just listened to me breathe, poked a swab around in my throat, and walked his fingertips along my neck where it hurt. Then he washed his hands and sat down to write out a prescription.

"You can sit in the chair now," he said, motioning me down from the examining table, where my legs dangled uncomfortably. When I was seated opposite him, I noticed that we were almost on eye level. I was almost as tall as he was!

"Well, Emily," he began mildly, "we won't know till the lab tests come back, but I'm pretty sure you have strep throat. I want you to rest, drink lots of fluids, and take this medicine. It will make you good as new in a few days." From behind his glasses he continued to survey me quietly. "Do you have any questions for me?"

I tried to think how to begin. My glance wandered around the room, then came to rest on his curly beard which was a mixture of gray and red. "Um, do I have to go to school?"

"No, I think you'd better take it easy till your fever goes down to normal," he replied. He continued to sit there as if he had all the time in the world. "How is school? Are you still getting all As?"

"Well, no," I spoke slowly, feeling suddenly ashamed. "I got some pretty bad marks the last few weeks." Then more quickly I said, smiling, "But I got the only hundred in the class on a big math test!"

"You got some bad marks and then you got a hundred," he repeated. "I bet your parents had a lot to say about that."

"No, they hardly noticed." I stared at my hands. "Mom's been so worried about Ben, she hardly has time for me." I felt as if I had waded into the ocean and decided to plunge in the rest of the way. "Doctor, what's wrong with Ben? No one will tell me anything! Will you?"

Dr. Bernstein blinked and paused a moment, uncrossing one leg and crossing the other. *He's deciding whether to tell me what my parents had kept secret. Please...* I said with my eyes. *You're my last hope.*

"Your brother has ADD, which means attention deficit disorder," he began.

I interrupted immediately. "I know, but how bad is it? Do people die from it...like a brain tumor?"

"No. It's nothing like that." He continued to watch me closely. "Were you worried that your brother was going to die?" he asked calmly.

I nodded miserably, my eyes filling with the tears I'd been holding back for weeks. My throat felt tight, reminding me of the soreness of the past few days. I kept my eyes fixed on his brown loafers and took a deep breath.

"What is ADD?" I finally asked, then blushed because he had just told me.

"Attention deficit disorder," he repeated patiently. "Your brother doesn't have enough of certain chemicals his brain needs to help him pay attention and stay on task. He's also hyperactive — you know, always moving around and talking."

I wasn't sure what he meant by "staying on task," but something else was bothering me more. "A problem with his brain? Will he be all right?"

"It's not like a brain tumor that makes your body get sick," he said. "It's a chronic problem that hangs around. We can give him medicine to make it less noticeable, but when the medicine wears off he'll still have it...unless he outgrows it. Oh, and by the way, Emily, you can't catch it from him, in case you were worried about that.

"How is it having Ben for a brother?" he went on. The question hung between us while I considered everything he was telling me. I still wasn't sure what ADD was, but at least I knew what it wasn't and that neither of us was going to die from it. I let out a little sigh of relief.

"What did you say?" I asked.

"How is it having Ben for a brother? Do you play together a lot? Do you get along most of the time?"

I hardly knew what to say. No one had ever asked me what I thought of Ben; they just told me what *they* thought. I remembered the chorus of criticizing voices from the dream two nights ago. "No, we hardly ever play together. He's pretty touchy and we argue a lot. He's usually in some kind of trouble, and so I try to get him out of it when I can." I remembered the backpack incident. "But sometimes I get in trouble instead."

"That must make you mad," he said. "And it's a pretty big responsibility looking after a younger brother — especially if he's always in trouble as you say." He made it sound as if it were perfectly okay to feel bothered about such a thing. I sighed with relief and glanced into his kind eyes, which held no accusations. He seemed to know more about how I felt than I did.

"Well, Emily, things should get better around your house now that we know what's troubling Ben. He's taking some medication to help him settle down, and maybe it will make him easier to get along with. I want to see you when your medicine is all gone." He stood up. "I'm going to go find your mother while you get your shoes and coat on." I fought the urge to run after him and give him a grateful hug.

Mom must have been right outside the door, because I heard him say to her, "Mrs. Clark, Emily has a bad infection, probably strep. You should have brought her in sooner."

She started to say something, but he went on. I'd never heard him interrupt anyone before.

"I know you're concerned about Ben, but your daughter needs you, too. In her own way, she's suffering just as much as you are over this whole thing. ADD can be very hard on siblings." Their voices were lost in the office noise as they walked down the hall.

# Chapter 11

When I got out to the waiting area, Mom was nowhere in sight. After a while she came out of a room down the hall, with Dr. Bernstein following her. "Here, Emily, this is for you. It might help you understand more about Ben. And we can talk more when I see you after your medicine is gone. Take care of yourself."

I smiled gratefully at him and glanced down at the flier he handed me. "Understanding Attention Problems," it said. *I hope it makes more sense than that book Mom was carrying around with her.* I'd stolen a peek at her book one evening when she wasn't looking, but it used lots of big medical words that hardly sounded English to me.

The car felt cold and silent after the warm, bustling office, or maybe it was just that I hated to leave the only person who seemed to understand me. I glanced sideways at Mom as she started the car. Would she treat me any differently after what Dr. Bernstein had said to her?

She cleared her throat. "Emily, honey," she began. "Things have been pretty difficult around our house lately, and I guess I haven't been paying much attention to you." She leaned her arm on the steering wheel. "I didn't explain ADD to you because I didn't understand it very well myself, and I didn't want to worry you. But I guess you knew anyway." She frowned, as if considering how I might have gotten the little bit of information I had.

"It was the books you were reading," I explained hastily. "I knew you were reading about some sickness, and when I saw you give Ben medicine, I figured he had something." I thought guiltily about listening through the grate and hoped that she wouldn't guess.

"Oh, the books, of course," she said. The puzzled frown disappeared, but her green eyes were still filled with concern. "Honey, I always count on you to be good, and you are. You're such a dear, sweet girl. I guess I take you for granted sometimes when I'm so busy with Ben, and now I've let you go without treatment for strep throat. I'm so sorry."

*Is that a hint of tears in her eyes?* "It's okay, Mom, I'll be all right," I said hastily, not wanting to make her sad.

"I guess Dr. Bernstein's right — all of us are suffering from ADD in one way or another — Ben because he has it, and you, Daddy, and me because we don't understand it." She took a ragged breath, and her voice quivered. "We'll get through it, honey."

Now I did see tears, I was sure. I looked away in embarrassment, but she patted my hand and said,

# I'm Somebody Too

"Emily." I turned back. "I love you, honey." She put her arms around me as much as she could with our seat belts holding us in place. I squeezed her tight, and her sweet-smelling hair brushed away my tears.

"I was so scared, Mom. I thought he had a brain tumor or something else really bad. I thought he was going to die. What will happen to him?"

She leaned back into her own seat. "He's not going to die, honey. It's not a sickness of the body, exactly. He's in perfect health — always has been, and he probably has more energy than Daddy and me put together!" She gave that joyless sound that passed for her laugh these days. "His brain doesn't know when to stop sending his body energy at night, and it doesn't send him the right amount to pay attention during the day. His brain gets mixed up. We have to help him."

"*How?" This isn't getting easier to understand, but it's so good having Mom talk to me about it, I don't care. Maybe it will make sense little by little, like math.*

"Well, Ben's psychologist suggested that we begin by making some charts to help him stay organized. I'll probably ask you to use them, too, to give him a good example."

She looked at me apologetically. "I know you're the most organized kid in the world and don't need charts, but will you go along with this to help us?"

Her praise settled inside me like a warm glow. "Sure," I said. At that moment I would've done almost anything she wanted. By the time we got home, I felt much better, even though I still had strep throat.

The medicine Mom gave me made me drowsy, and shortly after dinner I changed back into my nightgown. Next door I could hear Dad in Ben's bedroom, singing the same song I'd heard the other night. Mom brought the vaporizer to my room and read to me in bed for a while like she used to do when I was little. Even though I can read for myself now, it was wonderful to listen to her create the story for me with her own voice.

After a while I began to listen with my eyes closed and pretty soon the story seemed to fade away and leave only the message behind her warm words: "I love you, Emily." When I woke later to find the lights off and Mom and Dad's voices coming from the living room below, I just rolled over and went back to sleep. There was no need to listen at the grate tonight.

# Chapter 12

I got over my strep throat in three days. On the second day, Mary called to ask if she could bring me my homework; Mom said yes. I changed into the nightie I had gotten for Christmas, braided my hair, and straightened my room. Mary had never been here before. I pushed aside the white ruffled curtains Mom made me and leaned on the polished dark wood desk to watch for my friend. It was a bright, sunny day.

"Hi. You missed a spelling test and a new seating arrangement today," she said as soon as she came in.

"Where am I sitting now?"

"Third row, second from the back." Mary smiled happily. "Right next to me." Without waiting for my next question, she went on, "Ginny moved across the room next to Suzanne Featherstone, and Robbie Johnson's sitting right across from her! Suzanne was wearing lipstick, and she got caught passing a note to Ginny today."

*So it's finally happened like I knew it would: Ginny had moved away from me.* A couple of weeks earlier I would have felt terrible, but somehow it didn't matter so much now since I was sitting next to Mary. *In fact, it will be a relief,* I told myself firmly.

Mary turned around to make sure the door to my room was closed. Then she asked quietly, "How's your brother? He doesn't look sick to me."

"Oh, he's not. He doesn't have a brain tumor." She returned my joyful smile. "I mixed that up with what he really has — ADD, which stands for attention deficit disorder. My doctor gave me this pamphlet that tells about it."

"Oh, I've heard of ADD," Mary said. "My younger cousin has it, and he started taking medicine for it a couple months ago. When the medicine wears off, he acts like a real pain in the neck, but otherwise he's okay." She made a face. "For a boy." I laughed.

Mary looked at the pamphlet Dr. Bernstein had given me to read. "Yup, that sounds like how my cousin was until last year. My aunt was always yelling at him, and whenever he came over to our house my mom was a nervous wreck."

"Really? My mom's always a nervous wreck. She yells at Ben all the time. Everyone does."

"But you said he started taking medicine, right? My aunt said that helped my cousin a lot. Maybe it will help Ben, too," Mary said, laying the pamphlet on the bed and walking over to the bookcases built into my wall. "Boy, you sure have a lot of books."

"Yes, my mother's a librarian at the college. She gave me the complete set of The American Girls

Collection for my birthdays and Christmas and Valentine's Day. Don't I look like an old-fashioned girl?" I said, lifting one of my braids.

"You sure do," she said appreciatively. "And this whole room does, too. All you need is a nice picture of a horse on the wall over there."

"Mom just brought home this book on French braids," I said. "But I can't make them in my own hair. Can I try it on you?"

She was across the room in a second. "Oh, would you? I've always loved French braids. Some of the girls at the stable wear their hair that way, but I don't know how to do it." By dinner, when she had to go home, I had made a pretty good braid in her hair, and we went to show Mom.

"That's beautiful, girls," she said, looking up from the pot she was stirring. "Did you learn to do that from the book I brought you, Emily?" I nodded, and she smiled.

"I like the other books you gave Emily too, Mrs. Clark — The American Girls Collection. I've borrowed some from the school library."

"Well, maybe Emily will let you borrow some of hers sometime."

As Mary took her coat out of the closet, she brushed against the papers that hung from magnets on the refrigerator; a page drifted to the floor. She picked it up and glanced at it. "Ben's Morning Song," she read aloud. "Oh, my cousin who has ADD has something like this on his fridge too." I looked hastily at Mom, who raised her eyebrow but said nothing.

Mary handed the song to me and picked up her backpack. "You get better soon," she said as she went out the door.

"She seems like a nice girl," Mom said when I returned to the kitchen.

"She is, and I just got my seat changed today so I sit next to her."

Mom raised both her eyebrows this time. "What about Ginny?" she asked, stirring gravy. "I haven't heard much about her lately."

"Ginny's...she's sitting next to Suzanne Featherstone. She's hardly even talked to me since this new girl Melissa moved in and started coming to our school." The words rushed out of my mouth, and hearing them out loud made everything seem so real and final. *I really am losing my best friend.* I looked at Mom in wordless misery.

A hundred memories of Ginny in this room came flooding into my memory: Ginny following me through that door to wash hands for lunch and eating peanut butter sandwiches with me at the kitchen table; Ginny sitting next to me at the counter, both of us wearing paint shirts and fingerpainting; Ginny running beside me in the backyard, her silky golden hair blown back. I caught the sob in my throat.

Mom gathered me into her arms, and I let the grief come. "Ginny has changed so much, Mom," I said between sobs. "She acts like a stranger. She hangs around with the cheerleaders now and flirts with dumb old Robbie Johnson. She doesn't have any time for me anymore."

When I had stopped sobbing, Mom said quietly, "Everybody changes, Emily, especially at your age. Look at you, how tall you've grown." She picked up the end of one of my braids. "Remember when you were trying to grow your hair long?"

I nodded miserably, remembering Ginny and me combing our hair together, comparing how far it hung down our backs.

"She cut her hair now, and her friends wear lipstick."

Mom continued to regard me calmly. Suddenly I realized I wasn't used to having her talk to me for this long. *How come she's not yelling at Ben about his homework?*

"Where's Ben?" I asked.

"Your father is reading with him." Mom put down her book and smiled at me. "Want to play cards?"

We hadn't played cards since I-don't-know-when. I'd almost forgotten how. "I have to finish my homework," I said regretfully. Then I took a deep breath. "Mom, since I quit chorus, do you think I could take horseback-riding lessons with Mary instead?"

I couldn't believe I was asking her *that*. I'd been thinking about it for several days, but this moment, when I had her attention, was too rare to let pass.

Still, riding lessons were so expensive. I waited, hardly breathing, while she considered.

"Let me talk to your dad, honey," she said, "and then we'll see."

She hadn't said no! "Oh, thank you," I said, jumping up and hugging her. She laughed, and it was almost a giggle instead of the bitter "hmph" that had passed for her laugh lately. "I haven't said yes yet," she reminded me.

"I know," I replied, smiling to myself. "But maybe you will."

# Chapter 13

*Will I ever get used to Melissa sitting with Ginny on the bus and walking her into school in the morning,* I wondered the next day. I felt like I was wearing a sweatshirt that said "Extra Person: Not Wanted." *Can everyone see how miserable I feel being near the girl who isn't my best friend anymore?*

These gloomy thoughts made my boots feel two sizes too big as I trudged through the door to the school hallway. When I got to the door of our classroom, though, Mary was waiting for me. "Come on, I'll show you your new seat," she said. "Right this way, Ma'am," she continued, imitating a waiter in a fancy restaurant. Giggling, I followed.

Golden sunlight streamed through the blinds onto my desk; it was three rows closer to the window than before. "This is nice," I said in surprise, opening the lid to look at my stuff. Right on top of my books and papers sat a picture of a girl wearing a hard hat and white pants, clinging to a horse's mane as it leaped over a low white fence.

"*Equestrian* magazine," I read aloud, looking up.

# I'm Somebody Too

Mary smiled. "There's a poster inside that you can put up in your room," she said.

"Glad to see you back, Emily," said Mr. Miller as he walked by. "And how do you like your new desk, next to Mary?" His words were casual, but underneath I sensed that he really wanted to know how I liked sitting across the room from Ginny.

"It's fine," I replied, looking into his lively blue eyes. "See what she gave me?"

"A welcome-back present," he smiled. "Do you ride, Emily?"

"No, but I'm going to. Last night after you left, Mary, my parents said I could take riding lessons."

"Oooh, Emily!" squealed Mary. "You finally asked them!" Mr. Miller continued down the aisle, smiling.

"Hi, Emily. Were you sick?" I looked up to see Ginny standing by my desk, and told her about my strep throat.

When I was done she asked, "How do you like your new seat?"

"It's nice," I said.

"Well, even though we're not sitting next to each other anymore, we can still be friends." And before I knew how to reply, she had walked back to her desk across the room.

That afternoon when Mary corrected my spelling test, she drew a smiley face inside one of the zeroes of the 100% at the top of my paper. When recess came, Krissy Haynes asked Mary to swing one end of her long jump rope, and soon I was doing red-hot peppers. The chanting of the rhyme almost drowned out the cheerleading calls from across the parking lot.

As our class was lining up to go back into school, Ben's class came out. First I recognized his teacher and then looked for my brother at the end of the line, where he usually straggled four steps behind. Today, however, he didn't stand out. Instead, he was walking in the middle of the line, as if he belonged there. He met my eyes calmly as our classes passed each other. "Hi, Emily," he said, and kept going.

*Something seems odd about Ben,* I thought. *He never says hi to me first — in fact, he usually doesn't even see me.*

A few days later our whole family went to see a psychologist. Mom and Dad first announced it to us one night at dinner, saying, "We've all had quite a few arguments lately, and not as many happy times as we would like. We're going to see a psychologist, who can help us get along better."

"What's a psychologist?" I wanted to know.

"It's a doctor who asks you to do stupid things like reading words on cards and drawing things and putting puzzles together," said Ben, who had visited Dr. Lawson one day when I went to Mary's. "But it's not too bad. I didn't get shots or anything."

"How will *that* help us get along better?" I asked, confused.

"That's what Dr. Lawson did to find out how Ben

learns and pays attention," replied Mom. "But when we all go to see her, we'll probably just talk."

Dr. Lawson's office was much different from Dr. Bernstein's. There were no *Highlights* magazines or crying babies. *I guess babies don't usually go to doctors to learn how to get along,* I thought, *because there are no toys, either.* I passed over *Psychology Today,* which used big words like the books on ADD that Mom read, and settled on *People*; Dad picked up *Shutterbug.* Mom was reading a book to Ben when a slender black woman opened the door.

"Mr. and Mrs. Clark, you may come in now. Hi, Ben." Turning to me, she said, "And you must be Emily." *What does she know about me besides my name,* I wondered.

"I'm going to talk to your mom and dad for a little while first," Dr. Lawson said. "You two may come into our playroom. Emily, you may bring your magazine if you like."

The playroom had some stuffed animals in it and a wooden dollhouse. *I guess kids do come here after all,* I thought, looking around. *What's that weird window you can't see out of?* Ben put his face right up to it.

"What are you doing?" I asked.

"You can see Mom and Dad if you get close enough," Ben replied, "and hear them, too."

Dr. Lawson came into the room. "Ben," she said, almost laughing. "Please play with some of the toys until we call you. Leave the window alone." Then Ben dumped out the round container of farm animals, and by the time she called us in, he had them all mixed up with the cars.

Dr. Lawson ushered us into an ordinary-looking room with lots of comfortable chairs and plants. It wasn't as bright as Dr. Bernstein's; no examining table, either, and not a nurse in sight. *This sure is going to be different,* I thought, waiting a little nervously to see what would happen next. Dad winked at me.

"Now, I have already talked to everybody in the family except you, Emily," she began, looking at me. "Let's start with your age. How old are you?"

"Twelve. Well, almost."

She smiled. "And where do you go to school?"

"Northwood," I replied.

"Do you and Ben ride the bus together?" she asked, writing.

I nodded, wondering what that had to do with getting along.

"Do you sit together on the bus? Or do you each ride with your own friends?" Like many times before, I felt the heaviness in the bottom of my stomach whenever I thought of Ginny and Melissa, but this time, I realized, it was a little lighter. *I better pay attention — she's asking questions about Ben and me, not about my friends.* Pretty soon I was telling her about the time I grabbed Ben's backpack for him and then he wouldn't carry it home and I got in trouble.

"It's a pretty big responsibility being a big sister, isn't it?" said Dr. Lawson. "And what kinds of things do you two enjoy doing together?"

I looked at Ben, who stared at the floor. *We hardly do anything together,* I realized. *Some family.*

After a moment of silence, Dr. Lawson continued, "Well, what special things do the four of you like to do together?"

Mom and Dad looked at each other, frowning in concentration. Finally Mom answered, "A lot of our weeknights are taken up with homework. And I guess we each have our own hobbies that we do by ourselves. Sometimes we go to the museum or for walks in the woods, but we usually don't stay very long. As I told you." She looked at Dr. Lawson as if they had talked about this before.

The doctor nodded and made a few more notes. She asked about homework and whether we had chores, and that brought back stories of times when Mom was yelling at Ben and I was scurrying to do everything right to make her feel better.

"So you help your mother a lot by doing as you're told and by helping Ben when she's not around," Dr. Lawson said after awhile. Ben scowled at me, and I was afraid to answer.

Then we talked a little about what each of us likes to do in our free time. I was surprised to hear Mom say that she likes to paint. I had never seen her do it. Dad told her about his cameras and bird feeders, which I already knew about because he was always taking pictures when we went for walks.

By the end of the meeting, Ben and I had agreed to do our chores the first time we were asked (which I always did anyway) and Mom and Dad agreed to plan something fun for the whole family. Since that's all we accomplished, I was pretty steamed up about missing an afternoon at the horse farm. *Why do all of us have to go these dumb meetings to fix Ben?*

# Chapter 14

*Horses are higher and wider than they look,* I thought as I struggled to swing my knee over Shasta's broad back. For my first lesson, I was alone in the ring with two dogs and the trainer, Nanette. "Isn't there a knob or something to hang onto?" I asked.

"You're thinking of the horn on a western saddle," replied Nanette, a dark-haired woman in an old ski hat and jacket. "English saddles don't have horns. You'll do most of your hanging on with your knees, and you can also hold onto the saddle itself."

*How can I keep from falling off by just using my knees,* I wondered, but obediently grasped the front of my saddle and felt the warm blanket next to Shasta's neck. *This is really happening to me,* I thought, glancing over my shoulder to the outside of the ring, where Mary stood watching. She smiled and waved. Mom and Ben sat behind the glass in the observation gallery upstairs.

After making my stirrups the right length, Nanette showed me how to steer the horse around the fences — jumps, she called them — scattered around the ring. "Now, guide her out to the outside rail and walk," she directed. Shasta, who had other plans, lowered her nose to sniff the dog who had wandered up to us. I waited. "Squeeze your knees together and ask her to go," Nanette said to me, then clucked to my mount.

The horse started to walk around the ring, and as I shifted back and forth in the saddle, I became uncomfortably aware of bones in my seat that I hadn't ever known about before. When we got to the curved end of the ring, the horse started to take a shortcut to the other side instead of going all the way around the wall.

"Eyes straight ahead, and open your rein to the left," said Nanette. "Don't let her get away with that. Tell her where *you* want to go."

I pulled the reins toward the wall and, to my surprise, the horse yanked back. With all my strength I pulled harder, and Shasta simply stopped. "Squeeze your legs together, Emily, and ask her to go," repeated the trainer.

The first lesson lasted only a half-hour, but when I dismounted, I wondered how long it would take for my legs to feel like my own again. Surely the inside of my thighs had stretched permanently. Would those bones in my seat ever stop being sore?

My discomfort faded, however, when Mary met me by the stall. "You did great!" she said, sliding open Shasta's door. She patted the horse's nose. "Yes, you're a good girl," she said. "You and my friend are going to do just fine."

The next week I joined Mary's class. Nanette kept up a constant string of instructions and compliments as we rode around her in a big circle. Once we were riding around the ring, I was amazed how well I could always hear the trainer's voice, even though she never seemed to shout.

"That's good, Alison. Keep your heels down. Mary, give him a squeeze to keep him going. Sarah, don't let Spicey get so close to another horse. Remember, he doesn't like to be near anyone else. Cut across the ring so you're by yourself."

After a few more trips around the rail at a walk, Nanette told us all to stop. "Now, Emily, we're going to pick up the pace to a trot. Just have Shasta follow the horse in front of you, and hang on with your legs." When she clicked her tongue, the horse and rider ahead of me took off.

I clutched the saddle anxiously as my horse bounced me up-down, up-down in rapid succession. I felt myself slipping from one side of the saddle to another. And oh, those bones in my seat! Glancing ahead, I saw Alison gliding gracefully along, moving up and down in time to the horse's stride. She wasn't hanging onto anything except the reins!

"Good, Emily," Nanette said. "Now squeeze your legs together and keep your heels down." Doing as she said helped me stop slipping from left to right. Now if only I could quit bouncing so much!

"Mary, eyes straight ahead. Keep your head up. Lisa, good heels. Emily, now stretch up out of your saddle, and try to bounce down only once for every time you go up." I stretched up and down as she said, feeling a little silly doing knee bends on a horse's back. "That's right, Emily, now do it faster. That's it!"

Her voice faded away. Suddenly I felt as if I were floating above Shasta. *I've adjusted to her rhythm,* I realized, astonished. Up-down, up-down, round and round the ring. Every time I stood up in the saddle, I felt like a graceful circus rider stretching up toward the top of the tent. My hair streamed behind me and I felt myself growing warm with exertion, despite the chill of the unheated barn.

The bones in my seat didn't matter anymore; nothing mattered except the perfect, smooth rhythm. "Good, Emily! Now you're posting," said Nanette. I laughed aloud, glad to be alive. My whole being felt full of joy, and the feeling stayed with me all the next day, despite the discomfort in my legs and seat.

Two days later we got six inches of snow, so our family did something fun all together like Dr. Lawson had been telling us to do.

"Let's go sledding when Daddy gets home," Mom said when we walked in the door.

*Did I hear her right? Usually the first thing she says when we come in the door is, "Hang up your coats. How much homework do you have?"*

# I'm Somebody Too

"Yeah!" said Ben, slicing the air with an enthusiastic flourish.

Mom gave Ben another pill — I noticed she'd been doing that all week after school — and mentioned the H word. "Let's get homework out of the way so we'll have more time to play tonight." She sliced a few apples and put them on a plate on the table for us to snack on while we worked.

I eyed the fruit warily. *If I sit here and eat those apples, I probably won't get any work done because of all the fuss Ben will make about doing his homework. And I have a book report due in two days.* But the sunlight bathing the kitchen and my mother's nearness lulled me into giving it a try, despite the cautious feeling inside. I pulled up a chair at the table across from Ben and got out my novel and books. Taking a bite of apple, I resolved to ignore Ben if necessary.

Halfway through copying over my book report, I noticed that Ben was getting up from the table and Mom was smiling. Smiling! "That's the quickest you've ever done your math, Ben. Give me five." She put her palm up and he slapped it obligingly. "If you will get everything ready for the morning now, we'll have the whole evening to spend sledding. That is, if Emily ever gets done with her homework."

"If *I* ever get done!" I cried, not bothering to hide my hurt. "I have a lot more homework than he does. Besides, *I'm* usually the first one done."

Mom laughed and said hastily, "It was a joke,

# I'm Somebody Too

Emily. I'm sure you'll be finished."

"Oh." *What is happening to Ben and Mom? They seem so different, so...peaceful. Happy, even. There was none of the usual arguing this afternoon.*

Ben was halfway upstairs when Mom called, "Come back and look at your evening chart, Ben, so you can get ready for morning."

I winced and went back to my book report. *Such baby stuff, these charts.* The repetitive melody I had heard Dad singing had become a "Morning Song" with the most stupid lyrics I'd ever heard: "Clothes, hair, shoes, and backpack, lunch; clothes, hair, shoes, and backpack, lunch; clothes, hair, shoes, and backpack, lunch; that is what I do." It went to the tune of "Oats, Peas, Beans, and Barley," which I had learned in kindergarten.

We were supposed to sing it in the morning to remember all the things we needed to do before breakfast. Then there was another great verse for after breakfast: "Clean the table, wash my face, get my coat and get my boots, grab my backpack, give a kiss, that is what I do." *Disgusting.*

I wanted to throw up every time Mom asked us to sing it, but of course, I had to go along so Ben would learn from my example. But I didn't need the Morning Song — I did all those things every morning because they made sense. How could you go to school without your boots and your lunch?

When I had objected privately to Mom about

singing such a babyish song, she replied, "I know you don't need it, Emily. But a lot of things that make sense to you *don't* make sense to Ben. He doesn't see patterns easily."

"What do you mean by patterns?" I asked, puzzled.

"The pattern is the why behind a series of things that you do," she explained, brushing her bangs out of her eyes as she leaned on the counter. "Why do you put on your clothes and comb your hair before going to school?"

"Because I can't go to school if I'm not dressed," I replied, sighing. This question-and-answer game was almost as irritating as the song itself.

"Right. And why do you take your backpack and, in the winter, wear your boots?"

"Because I'll get yelled at by my teacher if I don't have my homework and won't be allowed to go out for recess if I don't have my boots. Really, Mom."

"What do getting dressed and taking the right things to school have in common?"

"Those are all the things I need to be ready for school," I said.

"Exactly. And that's the pattern. When you know the pattern, you just automatically think of the things you need to make it complete, right?"

"Right," I replied, tired of the whole conversation. "So what's the difference whether I get my backpack ready before breakfast or after? I won't forget it."

"Exactly," she smiled. "You know when things are

missing from the pattern, and you automatically do whatever you need to make it complete. You get the missing thing—your shoes or backpack, or whatever. But Ben has never figured out what he needs to get ready for school, so he never does those things on his own. I hope that the song will help him realize what he has to do without being told. But till he understands the pattern, the song will remind him — and *I* won't have to."

She looked out the window and smiled to herself. Then she met my eyes again and said, "It's working, you know."

"What do you mean?"

"Haven't you noticed that Ben is doing better? He's getting his work done more quickly and with less arguing."

"Well, yeah. I thought there was something strange about him. Is that all because of the Morning Song and the evening chart?" I asked, interested again.

"No. We're doing many other things, too, like working with his teacher so he has more appropriate assignments. Mrs. Lewis has modified Ben's spelling list, for one thing; and the medication is helping him pay attention," Mom said seriously.

I wasn't sure what "modified" meant, but I had a more important question. "How long must we continue going to Dr. Lawson?" I asked. "I can't see how it's doing us any good." Visiting her office kept me away from the stables because I had to do my homework before Dad got home.

"Dr. Lawson is going to help us all adjust to being a more normal family," Mom said briskly. "Doing fun things and...and having conversations like this." Her eyes gleamed when they met mine. "We're talking a lot more than we used to, aren't we, Emily?"

"Yes," I told her. To myself I added, *But it's still all about Ben.*

# Chapter 15

As Mom and I expected, I finished my homework by the time Dad got home. After a quick dinner, as we all suited up for sledding, I saw Mom put on red snowpants I had never seen before. They didn't match her pink jacket at all.

"I didn't know you had snowpants, Mom," I said.

"They're warm-up pants from skiing, back when I was in college. Your father and I used to ski a lot before we had you."

I paused to consider my mom and dad rushing down the slopes, carefree and laughing. I couldn't picture it, especially Mom.

Ben and Mom were still pulling on their gear when Dad said energetically, "I'm ready. I'll get the sleds. Come on, Emily, give me a hand."

"Where are we going?" I asked when he opened the double garage door. A couple of years ago we had gone sledding at Mendon Ponds Park, but that was at least a forty-five minute drive.

"How about over on the golf course?" he replied. "I bet they have some great hills over there." Behind the houses across the street I could see the rolling hills of the golf course, and I hoped the woods beyond had slopes long and steep enough for a good ride.

"We can cut through these yards," Dad said. "I'm sure our neighbors won't mind."

"But Larry," Mom protested to him, "we never even introduced ourselves when they moved in last summer. Let's go around."

Falling into step beside her, Dad said, "Look, it's six-thirty and it's just getting dark. Spring is on the way. This could be our last big snow for the season."

Pretty soon we were pulling our sleds across the unbroken snow of a wide field. "Why is the snow different here?" asked Ben. "Look, in this circle it's not so deep."

"That's my Eagle Eyes," Dad chuckled. "The grass is shorter underneath, too. These flat, rounded areas are called greens."

"What do you mean by 'Eagle Eyes'?" I asked him.

"Oh, Ben and I were talking about how he notices everything, kind of like an eagle." I felt a stab of jealousy, wishing I had a strong nickname like that.

I walked beside Dad in silence. By now it was almost dark. The lights of the houses looked far away, and the only sound was a gentle breeze that lifted my hair to brush my cheek. Inside my layers of sweater, jacket, and scarf I felt toasty warm with exertion, despite the cold, crisp air. I took a deep breath just for the joy of it.

# I'm Somebody Too

We followed a path through a wooded, hilly area. The moon through the bare trees cast sideways shadows on the forest floor, as if the ground were littered with fallen trees.

At the top of the hill, Dad stopped. "This should do," he announced.

Ben came up behind me. "Wow!" he shouted, looking down a long steep slope with no trees. "Can I go first?"

"Sure. Get on behind me," Dad said, plunking down on his sled and pushing off. I dropped mine next to them and caught my breath as the ground fell away beneath me. "Woah!" shouted Ben with delight as they plunged down ahead of me.

"Come on, Emily, we'll race you to the top," said Dad when we got to the bottom.

Mom was still at the top. "How was it?" she called.

"Great!" Dad replied. "Come on down." Still she stood at the crest of the hill surveying us below. *Why, she's scared!* I thought.

Dad handed the sled rope to Ben and scrambled up the hill by himself. "Want to ride with me, Nell?" She arranged herself carefully on the sled behind him, but once they began racing down the slope, she giggled and whooped like a girl.

Too soon, Mom announced that it was time to go home. I hung behind as we headed back across the expanse of snowy fields to the pine trees at the edge of the course. The quiet darkness felt soothing.

Dad waited for me. "Some morning I'd like to come out here and see if we can identify some of these animal tracks. Want to come along?" he offered.

"Oh, yes!" I said.

"Maybe we'll go on Saturday, if there's still snow," he continued.

"Hey, remember feeding chickadees at Mendon Ponds Park?" Mom asked.

"Yeah! That was great!" said Ben, next to her. "Can we go there again?"

As they chatted about the tiny gray birds eating out of our hands, I felt bitterness rise in my throat. *Everybody seems to have forgotten how Ben ruined that trip by scaring the birds away every time he got near me. He ran back and forth like an overexcited puppy reporting what he'd seen.*

*At least he's staying in one place tonight instead of running all around like he used to do,* I thought, listening to him chattering behind me. *But I wonder if he'll ever be quiet long enough to appreciate silence.* I slowed my steps until his voice seemed far away under the vast sky.

Mom walked back to me. "Having a good time, honey?"

"Yes," I replied. "I wish we could come back."

Back in our warm kitchen, Mom fixed hot chocolate for Ben and me and coffee for her and Dad. As I was going upstairs, they were heading for the living room, cups in hand. When I got into my bed, their voices came perfectly clear through the grate.

"Well, I hope Dr. Lawson will be pleased with our family outing," Mom said. "That was fun, although I wish I could make the sled go where I want it to go." Dad explained how to drag your hands to steer, then said teasingly, "I haven't seen you in those old snowpants in ages. Remember the first time we went skiing and you fell off the T-lift?"

"Don't remind me," Mom laughed. "I'm glad Emily is more coordinated than I am. She's doing quite well on her horse."

After a pause Dad said, "Ben seems better to me. What do you think?"

"Definitely. I think the medicine is working. But you know, I wish you would've gotten home earlier. You're always so late that it's hard to do anything together in the evening."

"You never *wanted* to do anything together in the evenings, remember?" Dad protested.

"I would love to do more things as a family," Mom said longingly. "Remember the time we went to the museum in Chicago and spent the whole time in the torpedo room because that's where Ben wanted to be? Then there was no time for us to see the famous dollhouse. I was so disappointed."

*So was I. And I can think of a million other times just like it.*

"Well, as Dr. Lawson said, we need to create happy times to replace the bad memories," Dad reminded her. "Tonight was a good start. And that reminds me, when are you going to take a course like she recommended?"

"Oh, Larry. I don't see how you'll manage during the evening."

"Doctor's orders," he said, somewhat teasingly. "She said it would be good for you, so go get the flier from the town recreation department, and let's decide which night. I'll come home early if I have to."

# Chapter 16

That Saturday, Dad and I set off right after breakfast. Big fluffy flakes brushed my face as we stepped out the side garage door into the yard.

"If we have to have snow in March, it might as well be deep," said Dad. "Seems like we're making up for those warm spells in January and February."

"Everyone else must have stayed in bed this morning," I observed, pointing to the unbroken view of snow in front of our house. Not a footprint marred the perfect landscape as far as I could see. Our street hadn't been plowed yet, either, so I couldn't tell where the pavement left off and the grass began. White sky, white snow...and silence.

Or what I took for silence. As I listened more intently, I heard the first of many birds twittering. "Birds!" I said. "They'll be hungry now that everything is covered by snow, won't they?" I asked Dad.

"No, I filled the feeders last night," he replied. "Let's go watch."

Fifty paces away, about twenty birds waited impatiently for their turn at the feeder. The small brown bird that pecked so hungrily was frightened away by the male cardinal, large and important with his bright red feathers. Soon his plainer mate came and feasted also, while the other birds fluttered nearby, keeping their distance impatiently.

"The more aggressive get their fill," Dad said, "and the others have to wait and take the leftovers." He laughed, then continued more seriously, "It's kind of like that with people, too. The squeaky wheel gets all the attention."

I nodded, wondering what he was trying to say. He crossed the street and cut through the neighbor's yard. "Your mother isn't looking and I'm sure they won't care," Dad explained, laughing mischievously.

"What I mean is this, Emily," he continued. "Ben, because of his ADD, has demanded a lot of your mother's and my time, and you've probably felt neglected." He paused and looked directly at me. I looked down at the snow. "But now that we know what's bugging him, we can get him in line. And I, for one, aim to make up for lost time with you."

Suddenly grabbing my hat, he raced away with it behind a giant pine tree and waved the hat like a flag, calling, "Bet you can't find me!" I giggled and set off to sneak up behind him, remembering games of hide-and-seek we had played when I was much younger.

Though the fluffy new snow muffled my footsteps, he turned when I approached. His blue eyes twinkled as he taunted, "Come on, Emily. Surely a strong girl like you can catch an old man like me!"

I lunged at him, but my arms grabbed empty air. He was off again, waving my hat on a stick over his head. Just when I had almost caught him, he swerved and doubled back on himself. Pulling myself up short in an effort to change direction, I plunged headlong into the snow.

He came over and tossed the hat to me. "Emily! What are you doing sitting there in the snow without your hat on? Shame on you!" he scolded teasingly, pulling the hat down over my hair and then over my eyes. "There. Now you'll be nice and warm." By the time I emerged from under my hat, he was standing about ten feet away. "We're playing tag and you're it," he said. And so it went. I never caught him and finally begged for a truce.

"Mom tells me you have a new friend," he said casually as we doubled back on our own tracks toward home. "Is it a girl...or a boy?" An exaggerated leer accompanied this last question. I laughed.

"Oh, Daddy," I began, falling back on my child-hood name for him, "I don't have boyfriends. I'm not pretty like Ginny. She has Robbie Johnson eating out of her hand."

"Ginny *is* a pretty girl," he said thoughtfully. "But I prefer someone with a little more color and nerve myself."

*"Color and nerve" sure don't describe the woman you married,* I thought to myself. *She was afraid to*

*come down the hill on a sled by herself.* Aloud I said, "You mean someone like Mom?"

"Oh, I didn't mean to marry," he said, his eyes twinkling. "I mean to walk with in the snow. But your mother and I used to have a lot of fun when we were first married. I bring out the daring side of her and she...she helps me think about lots of things. Kind of gives me a different perspective, you know?"

"How come you don't have fun anymore?" I asked, wanting to hear more.

"Well, Emily, when Ben got to be about three, he really started to be a handful. Mom was home all the time with him and became so frustrated, not knowing how to get him to mind her. At first, I didn't believe her and kept saying 'He's just a boy, he'll outgrow it.' But after awhile he got on my nerves, too, so I stayed away more and more...you know, spent a lot of time working in my darkroom.

"We felt we couldn't go anywhere because Ben would create such a fuss if he didn't get his way," Dad continued with a sigh. "Your mother has gotten worn out trying to manage both of you single-handedly, and I'm afraid it's taken all the fun out of her." He looked thoughtful, then determined. "Temporarily. I intend to fix *that* situation, also — to bring the sparkle back to your mother's eyes."

*While you're at it, please bring back her laugh,* I pleaded silently.

# Chapter 17

The next time we went to see Dr. Lawson, Ben and I got a chance to talk right away. Well, mostly, Ben did. "Last week I asked you to find something fun to do as a family," she began. "Emily, what did your family do?"

"We went sledding on the golf course across from our house," I replied. Then Ben interrupted to explain exactly how to get to the hill where we sledded, how high the hill was, and what kind of sled he used.

She said, "Sounds like you have more time to do fun things than you used to, Ben. Are you still getting your homework done?"

"Oh, yes," he answered happily, "and I got most of my spelling words right on the test."

Dr. Lawson looked up at Mom for a moment before continuing. "That's good! And how have your mornings been lately, getting ready for school?"

I looked at the beach scene in the picture over her desk while he told her in boring detail all about the Morning Song. She laughed when he sang it, with Dad chiming in when Ben forgot the words. Through the mini-blinds at the window, I could see dusk stealing the afternoon light. *I wish I were outside or at home or the stable — anywhere but here listening to Ben babble on like he always does. Nothing has changed for me.*

"Emily, Ben answered the question I asked you," Dr. Lawson said, "so here's another. How did *you* like the sledding?"

*So Dr. Lawson is on my side after all.* I wanted to say something really interesting, but I was afraid if I told her what was really on my mind she would think I was bad.

"Fine," I said lamely.

"Did you do any other fun things together?" she persisted.

"Well, yes," I replied carefully. "Dad and I went out for a walk on Saturday morning." I looked up at him, and he smiled with his eyes twinkling as he remembered too. Dr. Lawson caught the look.

With her gentle encouragement, I told her about watching the birds at the feeder and chasing my father around in the snow. I didn't tell her what Dad said about Mom, though. "It was kind of like when I was a little girl," I finished.

"When you were a little girl, you used to play more with your father?" she asked.

I nodded.

"Why did you stop?"

"I don't know," I said. "I guess each of us was busy doing our own stuff." *He was always hiding in his*

I'm Somebody Too

*darkroom or watching TV,* I wanted to say, then felt guilty for thinking such a mean thing.

Then Dr. Lawson said she wanted to talk to Mom and Dad by themselves, so Ben and I went back into the playroom. I took a piece of gum out of my purse and started unwrapping it.

"Can I have some?" Ben asked.

"No," I refused, still feeling mad because he'd done most of the talking about sledding.

"Come on," he insisted, reaching for it, but I held it as far away from him as I could. *You should stop this,* a voice said inside. *It will turn into an argument. You know Ben can't take no for an answer.*

Suddenly I felt the angry part of me take over, and I didn't care if I made Ben mad. I popped the gum into my mouth, and Ben pulled my hair, although not enough to really hurt.

"Ow!" I cried loudly. "Stop pulling my hair!" I jabbed him in the ribs with my elbow, and he yelled, too. Mom came in.

"What's going on in here? Can't you two get along for a few minutes?"

"He pulled my hair," I said in a hurt tone, knowing she'd believe that Ben started the fight.

Mom glared at him. "Ben, cut it out. Sit on the other side of the room until we finish," she said sternly, then closed the door behind her.

I smirked at Ben, then took another piece of gum out of my purse, unwrapped it slowly, rolled it into a ball, and put it in my mouth, smacking my lips. I felt powerful.

"Please, Emily," he said. "I have some gum at home. I'll pay you back."

*He's offering a trade instead of just demanding what I have!* I realized, almost giving in. Then I thought of how everyone had smiled at him while he sang that stupid Morning Song. No one had ever praised me for going along with it.

"Stop bothering me!" I said, loud enough for Mom and Dad to hear. "I told you no, and that's it!"

Ben raised his voice, too. "Well then, you better stop teasing me."

"Don't look at my gum if it teases you. I can do what I want." I took out another stick and began to unwrap it with elaborate care. Ben lunged for it just as Dad opened the door.

"Dad, Ben won't leave me alone. This is my last stick of gum and he wants it."

"Ben, this is the second time today you've made a ruckus," Dad said sternly. "Go sit out in the hall until we're..."

"I didn't do anything, Dad," Ben interrupted. "Besides, she started it."

Dad sighed. "I saw you grabbing for her gum, Ben. Now I don't want to hear any more about it. Go sit in the hall."

All the way home Ben sat with his back to me, arms folded, looking out the window. I hummed to myself, delighted with the wonderful way I had discovered to get even for all the times Ben had grabbed all the attention. *Ben has been the bad one so long, Mom and Dad will automatically think he starts arguments, even if he hasn't. I'll show them who's the good kid. Ben can't take that away from me.* I hummed a little more loudly.

"Shut up," my brother whispered under his breath. After a quick glance to be sure Mom and Dad weren't looking, I reached over and scratched his hand. He scratched back, hard.

"Ow!" I said loudly. "Leave me alone!"

"Benjamin!" Mom said, turning around. "I am sick and tired of all your arguing. You'll have to go to bed fifteen minutes early tonight. Now leave Emily alone!"

"But Mom, she started it," he objected again.

"ENOUGH, Ben!" Dad thundered. "That's what you always say." Knowing that Dad was right, Ben gave up and stared out the window again. I resumed humming just loud enough for Ben to hear. My plan was working.

*I'm Somebody Too*

# Chapter 18

After dinner a few nights later Dad said, "Emily and Ben, Mom is going to her first class in Chinese art. I'm going to help you with your homework tonight."

As Mom kissed us goodbye, Dad told her, "Nell, don't worry about a thing. Have a good time."

When she was out the door, he said, "How much homework do you have to do, kids?"

"None," I replied quickly. "I did all mine in school."

He nodded appreciatively. "Great, Emily. How about you, Ben?" I waited, sure that he would have to work all evening, like he usually did.

"Me neither," he replied. "Oh, Mrs. Lewis sent a note home for you."

As Dad scanned the note, Ben shifted anxiously from one foot to the other, then relaxed when Dad smiled. "Wow, Ben! Your teacher says that you did so well today you don't have any homework. Put it there, buddy!" They slapped hands, and Ben grinned.

"Since neither of you has homework, we can play a game of cards," Dad announced happily.

At first I felt disappointed that I wouldn't have my

father all to myself as I'd planned. Then I had a brilliant idea how to get what I wanted after all. "We have to pack our lunches," I said sweetly, taking the last cherry yogurt out of the fridge and stuffing it into my purple fabric lunch bag. *Now that I've taken Ben's favorite food, he'll have to fix a sandwich, but first he'll have to decide what kind. That should take him at least half an hour.*

"I'm done, Daddy," I said cheerily. "Want to play rummy?"

Dad looked uncertainly at Ben, who was still trying to find a lunch bag. "Sure. Come join us as soon as you finish, okay, Ben?" As we walked into the family room, I glanced over my shoulder to see my brother blowing air into the brown bag.

It wasn't hard to beat Dad at cards that evening because he kept checking on Ben as we played. Slapping the queen of hearts he discarded, I called "Rummy!" and placed it next to the nine-ten-jack that I had just laid down. But I didn't feel too happy about such an easy victory. I would rather have had a more interested opponent. Like a magnet, Dad returned to Ben's side in the kitchen as soon as I had won. My brother went to bed just before Mom got home.

"Well, hello, Madame Artist," Dad said breezily as she came in. "How was Chinese art?"

"Fine," she said, smiling, "and how did everything go for you this evening?"

"Everything's in order," Dad reported proudly.

"Neither of the kids had homework. In fact, Ben's teacher even sent a note home saying that he had done so well he didn't need to do any work tonight. He's gone to bed." *He didn't say how late Ben went to bed, I noticed.*

"That's great!" Mom said, beaming.

"And Emily and I played a game of rummy while Ben packed his lunch," Dad continued. "Did I leave anything out?"

"No, honey," Mom replied happily, lifting her face to kiss him.

When I got home the next afternoon, I couldn't wait to go outside. "Mom, can I walk to the stable? I'll be careful," I said.

"I'm sorry, Emily, but we're taking Ben to Dr. Bernstein in half an hour. But if we still have time after that, I'll take you to the store like you asked."

"Why do we have to go to Dr. Bernstein? Is Ben sick or something?"

"No, we just have to get Ben's medication adjusted," Mom replied, then smiled. "Lately you two have gotten your homework done and we've had lots of time to do things we like, haven't we?"

"Yes," I admitted reluctantly. *What she really means is that Ben doesn't putter over his homework so much now that he is on medication. Even I can see a difference. But what about me? I always get mine done on time, and no one ever congratulates me.*

"You've got a little time before we go. Why don't

you take a walk on the golf course instead?" Mom said pleasantly.

"Oh, all right," I grumbled.

"Wear your watch, and be back by four o'clock," she advised as I went to get my coat.

"I *know*," I said testily, then closed my mouth on the rest of what I wanted to say: *You don't have to tell me everything like you do Ben.*

A million diamonds seemed to glitter on the unbroken snow of the golf course, and the light breeze soothed my confused feelings a little. A few paces onto the wide field, I turned to glance back at my footsteps in what was left of the snow. My boot print looked so big — was it really mine? Nothing was familiar anymore. My best friend had changed, my brother was different, and my family was doing so much stuff together now that there was hardly any time to be alone and just think.

*Mom and Dad are really carrying this counseling thing too far. I used to have so much time in the evening to read and talk on the phone when Dad was watching TV and Mom was standing guard over Ben. Now one of them suggests something to do together almost every night.* "Emily, would you like me to try a new braid in your hair? Do you want to play cards? Let's all go out for a walk. How about helping me fill the bird feeder? Do you two want to bake cookies?" *The worst part is that Ben is always there, too, talking a mile a minute and saying things that make Mom or Dad laugh.*

# I'm Somebody Too

*It's as if a new person lives inside Ben,* I realized suddenly. He used to be in the wrong place at the wrong time, saying something to make everybody mad. Whenever he had been with his class at school or even with Mom, Dad, and me, he had always lagged several steps behind, as if he didn't fit.

I could usually count on him to be the last one ready — and that automatically made me first. Now I had to work harder to be first, and sometimes he beat me anyway. Oh, sometimes early in the morning or late in the day he seemed like the old Ben, forgetting things Mom told him and dawdling. But then she'd remind him of one of her many charts, and in a little while he'd be okay again.

Last week when Dad had showed him how to make snow angels, Ben tramped "I love you" into the snow with his boots. When we made chocolate chip cookies, he had suggested that we save some of the chips to make smiley faces. "What a cute idea!" Mom beamed.

The worst time was last Sunday, when Mom was catching up on some reading for her job. Ben took her cookies and milk on a tray.

I followed him into the living room when he carried in her treat. "Snack time!" he announced. She looked up and, as she took in what was on the tray, her eyes filled with happy tears. "Oh, Ben, how sweet!" she said softly. Quickly wiping her eyes dry, she gave Ben a big hug, and for once he didn't squirm away.

# I'm Somebody Too

Mom and Dad were both charmed with this new son, I could tell. Who wouldn't be? I stood behind him that day, not knowing what to do with myself. Finally I went back to my room while Ben sat next to Mom and talked about the birds he had seen at the feeder yesterday. She seemed pleasantly surprised that he remembered some of their names.

Later in the kitchen, Mom asked me to put away the warm milk and wipe up the crumbs because Ben was out playing. I wanted to ask, *What's so great about fixing a snack if you leave the mess for someone else to clean up?* But I kept silent, not wanting to spoil her new happiness.

# Chapter 19

The next time we had an appointment with Dr. Lawson, Dad brought a book on making birdhouses. "Planning to tell Dr. Lawson all about your feathered friends today?" Mom teased. I smiled in spite of myself. More and more, they were acting as if they enjoyed one another.

"No," he laughed. "I thought this would keep Ben busy while he's waiting."

Mom nodded appreciatively. "Good idea."

My parents talked to the psychologist first, and after about ten minutes they came out and called me in. When Ben got up to follow me, Dad stopped him, saying, "No, son, stay here. Just Emily for now." Passing Mom in the doorway, I looked questioningly at her, and she patted me on the arm.

Indicating the couch facing her armchair, Dr. Lawson said, "Make yourself comfortable, Emily." I admired her soft accent, wondering briefly where she had been born. "I thought it would be nice to speak to you alone today since you haven't had much of a chance to talk in the sessions with your whole family."

I looked up, surprised that she had noticed.

"Your family has been coming to see me for several weeks," she went on, "and now I want to get your impressions of how things are going."

"Okay, I guess. I mean, Mom doesn't yell so much and we've been doing more fun things," I said, trying to tell her what she wanted to hear.

"What else has changed?"

"Well, Dad is doing more stuff around the house and with us kids, and that makes Mom happy," I reported.

"How about Ben? Does he seem happier?"

"Sometimes," I said, meeting her eyes. She looked calm and interested. *I wonder if she would understand how this new brother is messing up my life. I'll try,* I decided, then told her the story about Ben's cookies and milk, and how I had to clean up after. She listened attentively without interrupting.

"And how did that make you feel when you had to clean up after he got all the credit?" she asked softly.

"Bad," I said. My throat hurt from trying to hold the angry words back.

"Can you say more about that feeling, Emily?"

"It's just not fair," I said haltingly. "All my life I've tried to keep everybody happy. When Ben loses his lunch money or forgets his backpack, I help him out. And I try not to let him bother me too much, although it's never much fun to be with him. When Mom is mad at him, I try to be extra-nice so she can be proud of at least one kid. Sometimes, though, she's so mad that she just ignores me when I try to do nice things for her, and that made me feel twice as bad."

"Kind of helpless?" she interjected.

"Right." I took a deep ragged breath, fighting the emotion inside. "Now Ben's taking some magic medicine that makes him nice for the first time, and Mom is falling all over herself with happiness. But she never really noticed how good I was all along!" My voice sounded thin and high with strain; I hoped she didn't notice the tears threatening to spill out onto my hot cheeks.

"It's not easy when the people you love change, even for the better," she observed softly.

"What do you mean?" I asked, trying to catch a tear before it escaped. Despite my effort, it slipped out anyway.

She handed me a tissue, saying, "Your family has been dealing with a very difficult thing, Emily, and didn't even know it. ADD can be *very* tough on families, and everybody works around it in the best way they know how. Your way has been trying to fix everyone else's life by being extra-good and never complaining, even when that was hard for you."

I nodded silently, hoping she would say more. She was telling my life story, and I wanted to hear every word of her version.

"Now that Ben is starting to get some positive attention at home, you're not the only good kid anymore. You don't know *where* you fit or if they even need you." I nodded vigorously, feeling my throat tighten as if I were going to sob.

"It must have been nice to be the kid who always makes her parents proud," she observed quietly. "You know, the one with no problems."

"No problems!" I cried, abandoning control of my angry tears. "I was really sick and Mom wouldn't even take me to the doctor because she'd taken so much time off from work for meetings about Ben. And I got so upset about losing my best friend that I failed a test. But Mom was too busy worrying about *him* to even notice!"

As I brushed the hot tears away impatiently, Dr. Lawson came and sat next to me on the couch. Putting her arm around me, she murmured, "It's okay, Emily. You have lots of angry tears to shed, and it's safe to let them out. Because things are going to get better, for you, too."

Even as I closed my eyes and fought back the sobs, I noticed the warm comfort of being understood. When I could talk again, I confessed, "I haven't been very nice to Ben lately."

"Oh, really?" she said, sounding unconcerned as she pulled another tissue from the box and handed it to me. "I'm sure you'll find a way to deal with that as time goes on." As she moved back to her chair, I straightened my clothes and dried my eyes.

Dr. Lawson looked at her watch. "It's about time

for us to stop today, Emily. Would you like to talk about these things again?" I nodded in reply.

"Good. In the meantime, I will give you a little homework. Naturally you'll do it because you're such a good girl, won't you?" She winked, and I laughed shakily. Taking a pink sheet of paper from her drawer, she said, "I want you to keep a list of things you're angry or sad about this week, okay? I'll show you how to get started."

Writing, she read aloud, " 'I am angry because I have to pick up after Ben. I am angry because Mom never notices me.' You see how easy this is? Fill up one or two pages if you can. You don't have to share it with anyone, but you may show it to me next week if you like."

After dinner a few nights later, Dad suggested that Mom go upstairs to read her new book on Chinese art. "Well, Ben has a diorama of Hawaii to finish tonight," she said doubtfully.

"That's okay," Dad said. "I'll see that he gets it done. Ben, do you know what you're going to put in it?"

"Yup," replied my brother.

"See? Leave it to me," Dad said confidently, shooing Mom out the door.

"Well, all right, if you're sure you can manage."

I finished studying for my spelling test and turned on the National Geographic special about the horses of Assateague. Dad watched it with me and read his magazine at the same time. During a commercial near the end, he called to Ben, "How's your project coming, son?"

"Fine," came the reply.

When the program was over, I clicked off the TV and started toward the stairs for my room, passing Mom in the kitchen.

"Come on, Ben, it's eight o'clock," said Mom.

"But I'm not done with my diorama," he objected.

"Larry, I thought you were supervising," Mom said accusingly. Dad rose from the couch and came in.

*Uh-oh,* I thought. *Here we go again.*

"I was," Dad replied. "He said he was doing fine. You almost done, Ben?" Dad said hopefully.

"Almost," said Ben. "I just need to have a couple more people to use as Hawaiians, and I'll be all done. Oh, and color some scenery."

"But Ben, that's *everything* you need to do to make a diorama. You haven't even started it yet." Mom looked angrily at Dad. "Is this how you supervise homework? And did he make his lunch yet? Or pack his backpack for morning?"

"Ben, what did Mom tell you? Go get your Hawaiians," Dad ordered. Ben hurried out of the kitchen.

"Thanks a bunch!" Mom said hotly. "Now, instead of helping Ben in the evening when I have time, I have to do it in the morning when I'm trying to get ready for work. Don't do me any more favors!"

"Nell, I'm sorry. He said he was almost done, and I knew he was on his medication, so I figured he could handle it." Well, at least Dad's honest, I thought, liking the way he stood up to her.

"Medication isn't magic, you know," she retorted. "It works best when we also have the structure to back it up. That's why I designed all these charts. Even though you didn't go to all the meetings at school and with Dr. Lawson, can't you at least follow through? Besides, the medicine has worn off by now; you'd realize that if you thought about it two seconds. And furthermore..."

I looked from one parent to the other, seeing their arguments from both sides, not knowing what to think.

"Look, Nell, I'm trying," Dad interrupted. "I really am. I cooked dinner three times last week and cleaned up the kitchen, and we went sledding and went to Dr. Lawson...and look how much better..."

The phone rang and I dragged the cord out into the hallway, shutting myself off from my parents' argument. To my surprise, it was Ginny asking for the math assignment. After chatting a few moments with her, I hung up and listened through the door. Dad was still trying to make peace. Apparently Mom wasn't satisfied, however, because she started yelling at him for the way he'd cleaned up the kitchen.

Ben was hanging out on the stairway, looking scared and uncertain, so I asked him, "Did you find your Hawaiians?"

"No, I had some people in my Legos, but they

aren't in my closet," he replied, "and Mom is real mad at me."

His blue eyes darted nervously as he swung back and forth on the railing. He looked so much like the lost kid he used to be that my heart filled with the old familiar pity.

"I saw your Legos the other day in the basement, by the laundry sink," I said kindly. "Do you have any construction paper I can use for scenery?"

"Yes, but I don't know what to color on it," Ben replied, kind of whining.

"Just do some palm trees and a volcano," I advised. "Go get your shoe box and I'll show you how."

"I can't go back in there! Mom and Dad will yell at me again."

*I don't blame him. They aren't even talking now. What are they doing?*

"Maybe they won't notice if you're real quiet. Go on, and I'll help you."

Ben returned right away.

"What were they doing?"

"Mom was cleaning the refrigerator and Dad was reading," Ben reported in a whisper.

We hurried up to Ben's room, and in five minutes the project was done.

"Now, just take your clothes off and get in bed before Mom comes in. If you pretend you're asleep, she won't say any more."

"Gee, thanks, Emily. You really helped me a lot."

"Don't mention it," I replied, secretly glad that he had. As I hung up my sweater in my own closet, the doll with two faces smiled vacantly at no one in particular, her head cocked to one side as she leaned sideways on the shelf. Mom must have pulled her out of the corner when she put clean clothes in my closet. I took the doll out and settled her on my dresser, happy side showing.

"That's right, everything's going to be fine," I told her. "Mom will get over being mad by morning, and when she hears how I helped Ben finish his project, she'll be grateful. You'll see."

# Chapter 20

The next morning I didn't wake up until Mom called me. Before I was even out of bed, she asked, "Emily, did you get your homework done last night?"

"All done," I assured her. "And Ben's done with his, too." I smiled, waiting for her to look pleased. But she looked puzzled instead.

"When did he do it?"

"I helped him last night while you were...talking to Dad." I was glad I caught myself before I said *fighting with Dad.*

"Oh, dear, I woke Ben early to help him get it done," she replied. "But thank you, honey. By the way, is your homework all finished?" she repeated absently, opening my curtains and peering out the window.

"Yes," I repeated patiently. She must still be thinking about her fight with Dad. "I checked everything off my assignment pad."

"Good. And did you make your lunch?"

"Um, no," I said, adding hastily, "but I know just what I'm going to have. I can do it real fast."

"How about your backpack?" she continued on her mental checklist. "Is it ready by the door?"

"Well, no," I admitted, not looking at her. *Now I'm in for it,* I thought.

"Emily, you know the Morning Song," Mom said heatedly. "You complained that you're too big for it, and yet you didn't even do it. I'm very disappointed. I guess no one thinks of a thing unless I'm here to remind them," Mom said resentfully, and strode out of the room.

I shut the door behind her, close to tears. I hadn't been able to make her forget about her argument with Dad after all, and her criticism of me felt all the worse because I'd been expecting praise. I spent the rest of the before-school time trying to please her by doing everything perfectly. Even Ben followed his Morning Song after I reminded him about it when Mom wasn't looking. But her tight-lipped control did not relax until just before she kissed us goodbye at the door.

I ran down the hill, glad to put distance between myself and the feelings in that house. The early April air felt gentle and fresh. "Wait for me," called Ben, racing behind me.

"She was pretty mad at you, too, wasn't she?" he said, a little out of breath.

"Oh, that was nothing compared to what she said to Dad last night," I said defensively, stopping and looking at him for emphasis. "And you started it. She wouldn't have said anything to him *or* me if you'd done your stupid diorama like you were supposed to do."

Heedless of the hurt in his eyes, I continued accusingly. "Mom and Dad are always talking about how much better you are now that you're taking your medicine. But I think you're just the same. You haven't changed a bit."

Stalking off ahead of him, I took my place in the bus line. Out of the corner of my eye, I could see him dragging his backpack along the gutter. Now he really looked like the old Ben; I had helped put him back in that place with my angry words. I felt awful and didn't talk to anyone all the way to school.

"Hey, Emily, aren't you even going to say hi?" said Mary, standing by my desk a half hour later.

"Oh, sorry, I didn't hear you," I replied.

"You look awful. Is something wrong?" she asked.

"Yeah, my parents had a big argument last night, and my mom was still mad this morning." I stared out the window.

"My parents argue a lot, but they get over it pretty fast," she offered consolingly.

"Well, mine *never* argue. And last night when I went to bed, they weren't even talking to each other." She shook her head sympathetically, and I went on, "So I helped Ben finish his homework, and this morning Mom yelled at me because I didn't have my backpack ready. As if it takes me any time to do that."

"Did you see 'The Horses of Assateague' last night, Emily?"

# I'm Somebody Too

Glad she'd changed the subject, I allowed myself to be distracted. As soon as I got home that afternoon, I asked Mom if I could go to Mary's on my bike. "Oh, Emily, I thought you might like to bake some cookies," she objected.

*She knows I love chocolate chip cookies; is she trying to make up for this morning?* Suddenly I was tired of trying to guess her moods.

"No thanks, Mom. Mary was going to show me a new book about horses." Throwing on a sweater and a spring jacket, I fled from the house as quickly as I could. I needed some fresh air to help me sort out my mixed-up feelings.

Gliding down the hill to Watson Road, I felt like the two faces of my doll were speaking at once. The smiling side seemed to be saying, "Help other people and make them feel good, no matter what it costs. And never tell people when you're angry or hurt, because then they will feel bad."

The frowning face seemed to say, "Who cares what they want? Did pleasing them ever get you what *you* want? When will it be time for Emily? You're somebody too — don't you deserve to be heard?"

Both voices seemed to speak the truth. But how could they both be right when they said opposite things?

"Which one of those voices is the real me?" I murmured to the wind. Its caress felt like an answer, but I couldn't make out what it meant. When I reached Mary's, I was glad to put those troubling questions aside for a while. Mary had a new puppy who loved to play catch and, once I got over my disgust at touching the wet ball, I became totally absorbed in the young animal's enthusiasm for the game. For the next three days, I thought of almost nothing but bikes, puppies, and horses.

That day, when we went to Dr. Lawson, Mom and Dad spent most of the time with her. Then it was my turn. "We have only a few minutes today, Emily, but I want to talk about your anger list. Did you bring it?"

*Of course I did; I've been waiting several days to show you,* I thought.

"This is very good," she said in her soft voice. "You are working hard on getting in touch with your feelings." I told her about Mom and Dad's fight and about Mom's not thanking me for helping Ben. Then I told her that I didn't really think Ben had changed that much.

"Oh?" she said. "Last week we talked about how he was different and you didn't have a place in the family anymore."

"Well, I guess I was wrong, because I can make him act like his old self. And then I'm the good one again." I said. It felt funny to say these things to someone else out loud.

"Does that make you feel better, knowing that things won't be different after all?"

"No." I hated to admit it, but it was true.

"Emily, sometimes when we are trying to make changes in our lives, we take three steps forward and two steps back. It's almost like March weather — just when we think it's spring, we get another snowstorm. But it usually melts quickly that time of year, just like we usually recover quickly from going backward. Could this be a temporary setback in your family?"

"Maybe," I said, wanting to believe her. "Everything seemed to be going better for a while. Ben and I even played checkers without having an argument. But you know what?" I said, looking sideways at her.

"What?"

I got brave and told her about the mean things I'd said to Ben, even though I half-expected her to chide me. "Sometimes that happens," she remarked mildly when I'd finished. "And how do you feel toward Ben now?"

"Sorry." I picked at lint on my pants.

"Could you tell him that?"

"Well, I guess so."

After reminding me I didn't have to say everything that came into my head, she told me to continue my anger list. "When you feel angry, it also helps to do something physical to express it, like slam doors or punch pillows or take a walk. Try doing some of those things this week, and we'll talk again next week."

Just before I opened the door, she said, "Sometimes when we are working on releasing our feelings, they come out in dreams. Don't be surprised if you have remarkable dreams this week. Think of them as friends trying to tell you something, and write them down for me." I left reluctantly, hugging my list of hurts and grievances close to me so no one else would see it.

That night I dreamed that a cloud of thick black smoke was filling up our kitchen. Groping for the door, I escaped outside into the twilight, only to have the cloud follow me. Soon it was filling up the whole world. I mounted Shasta and raced headlong into the blackness, bursting through the other side onto the golf course in the bright daylight. I rode like the wind, strong, unstoppable, and free.

# Chapter 21

I couldn't wait for my next riding lesson, remembering the powerful freedom of my dream and the joy I always felt when we did a posting trot. The feeling of oneness with the horse seemed to blot out everything else for a while. After several weeks of lessons, the bones in my seat protested with only a dull ache after I was finished.

As Mary and I strapped on our hard hats in the lesson office, she checked the chalkboard to see which horses we were riding.

"Hmmm, there's a new girl's name here, and she has Shasta. You have Beau this week."

Beau eyed me suspiciously as I led him from his stall. He was at least six inches taller than Shasta, the horse I was used to.

"Now Emily, Beau likes to get right up behind other horses," Nanette instructed. "But if you let him follow too closely, they'll kick him. So keep him at least one horse's length away." We started out walking our horses around the rail, and I kept a very safe distance from the pony ahead of me. Soon, however, my longer-legged horse had caught up to the pony again.

Beau reminded me of Ben when he wanted to watch television. Nothing could keep him away.

"Cut across the ring so you're by yourself," instructed Nanette. A few minutes later, she said, "Let's pick it up to a little posting trot," clucking to the horses. Halfway around the ring, I could see Mary and her mount gliding effortlessly along. Beau, however, wanted to continue walking.

"Squeeze with your legs, and give him a good kick," advised Nanette, clucking to the horse again.

Suddenly Beau bolted off faster than I had ever gone before. Unaccustomed to his speed and long stride, I slipped dangerously from one side of the saddle to the other, clutching desperately with my hands. Then I remembered my reins and pulled on them. "Woah." Just before we ran into the back of Spicey, Beau stopped so suddenly that I almost went over his head.

Once I had regained my balance, I let out a long breath and discovered that inside my light jacket I was sweating.

"Emily, you have to control the horse. You can't let him control you," Nanette repeated. "You're not giving him any directions, so he knows he can run away with you." *Just like Ben,* I thought. *Mom and Dad don't give him any direction, and he makes everyone do things his way.*

Suddenly I hated this horse and wished I'd never signed up to take riding lessons. It was too much like home.

I had trouble tearing myself away from these angry thoughts to listen while Nanette reviewed my earlier lessons about steering, stopping, and starting. I felt like I hadn't learned a thing since I'd started, but felt a little better when she continued. "Shasta is a smaller, slower horse," Nanette explained. "Beau is larger and faster, but he needs more direction. Show him who's boss. Now I want you to walk around the rail, keeping him out to the edge. Tell him where *you* want to go."

I had never had to do much to Shasta, I realized. She had just naturally wanted to go wherever she was supposed to. But Beau wanted to be right up behind the other horses, and started taking a shortcut across the ring to get there. When I pulled on my reins to guide him over against the wall, he stood stock still and yanked back.

"Squeeze with your legs and ask him to go." When I did as Nanette directed, Beau bolted into a trot, catching me unawares again. I slipped from side to side, clutching at my saddle.

"Woah. Woah!" called Nanette. "Emily, you must give directions to your horse and be ready when he follows them. Beau might as well have been running without a rider just now."

Embarrassed, I returned to the edge of the ring.

Glancing at my watch, I saw that the lesson was only half over. Always before, it had ended before I wanted it to.

But by the end of the hour, Beau and I seemed to reach some kind of understanding. He trotted when I asked him to and I kept my seat when he did so. By the time Nanette told us to slow it down to a walk again, I had managed to match my up-and-down movements to the horse's stride and enjoy a few moments of the harmony that I loved.

"So how'd you like Beau?" asked Mary when I got back to the stall.

"He's sure different from Shasta!" I replied. What I really wanted to say was, *Let me out of here.*

"I had Shasta at the beginning, too. She pretty much does whatever Nanette says. The only thing is, when you want to trot or canter, she doesn't go very fast. Wait till you really get Beau going. You'll love him." Her eyes sparkled as she pulled off her hard hat and shook out her hair. "Oh, I almost forgot." She reached in her jacket pocket and pulled out a small china horse, white with a flower woven into its mane.

"I got one of these from each of my aunts for my birthday last fall, and I didn't know where to take one back. Would you like to have it?"

"Oh, yes! Thank you!" About the size of my palm, the horse looked like it was trotting. "But I think I'll call it Shasta — not Beau," I laughed.

# Chapter 22

Was there no end to the childish exercises I had to do to help Ben get better? "We still need to work on being ready for school in the morning," Mom announced at dinner one night, "so I've made up some charts for you to use to remember everything you need to do." Her chart had "clothes, hair, shoes, backpack, lunch, wash your face, get your boots," just like the Morning Song. We were supposed to check off each thing as we did it.

"And at the end of the week, if we have enough check marks, I'll give you a reward."

"What kind of a reward?" Ben asked.

"Oh, I don't know. Something nice," Mom replied airily.

"Do *I* have to do it?" I asked.

"Yes, Emily." She gave me a secret look that said, *Be a good girl and help me teach this to Ben.* I sighed and went back to my peas, but inside I cried, *Can't you ever think about anything besides Ben?* The next morning, however, I sang the song and checked off each item on the chart, and Ben did the same.

"Good, Ben," Mom said approvingly just before we

went out the door for the bus. "I see you're all ready this morning with no problems."

Spring was really coming now; I could smell it on the April breeze. "Don't those rocks look sort of like a cougar ready to pounce?" asked Ben, pointing to the rock wall arching around us in a half-circle.

I looked where he pointed and wondered why I had never seen it before. "Yeah, kind of," I said.

"Pretend I'm the cougar and you're a horse," continued my brother. "The cougar wants to eat you." He ran along the wall behind me, nimble as the cat he pretended to be. With the wall arching around me, whichever way I turned, there he was. In my horse's mind I panicked and looked for a way out, but the cougar had already sprung ahead, blocking the path around the bushes.

Then he spread his arms and made a bird noise. "I'm an eagle, and I'll save you from the cougar." He swooped down on the cat, describing in graphic detail how he was crushing it with his talons and dropping it in the bushes.

Mom opened the front door and called, "Children, you'll be late if you don't hurry down to the bus."

"Now that the cougar is dead, we can go," said Ben, smiling triumphantly.

"My horse will race your eagle," I said, picking up my pace to my best trot. But trotting was awkward in a long coat, I discovered, as Ben ran ahead.

"Eagles can fly long distances without getting

tired," he called back to me. "Horses get tired."

"Yes, but horses can carry people on their backs, and eagles can't."

"That's true," he admitted, spreading his wings for a long curving flight back to where I was.

When we were walking side by side again, Ben asked, "Emily, what do you think Mom will give us if we get all stars on the chart this week?"

"I don't know."

He turned to me, his blue eyes dancing. "Probably a new chart," he said, laughing.

# Chapter 23

By the time spring had really arrived, things were so much better at our house that we stopped seeing Dr. Lawson for a while. It was just as well, because Mom and Dad took up their outdoor gardening where they'd left off two years ago. Ben was so eager to roam the nearby fields that he got his homework done as soon as he came home. And I spent many happy hours with Mary dropping stones into a creek and listening to my voice echo in the tunnel that carried the water under the road.

"Let's go somewhere fun today," Mom said a few weeks later on a Saturday morning in May.

The three of us looked up from our cereal in surprise. "Does this mean we won't clean the tool shed today as we planned to?" Dad asked hopefully.

Mom smiled sheepishly. "Well, I know how much I wanted for all of us to work on it...but it's so nice out today. Maybe we'll do it next time it rains."

I followed her glance into the backyard, where the tulips were blooming in the neat flower beds. In front of the pines at the back of our yard, a pink flowering

tree stood like a ruffle on a dress. The branches of the
maples looked thick with green leaf buds. Where all
had been gray six weeks before, now sunlight shone
through the branches, leaving a dappled pattern on
the new shoots of grass coming up everywhere.

"Yes!" said Ben. "Remember how I saw an eagle
last time we went to Birdsong Trail? Maybe we'll see
some again today. Maybe we'll see baby eagles. I
mean...maybe I will. You know..." He paused signifi-
cantly. "I'm Eagle Eyes. I notice everything."

Mom smiled fondly at him, even though we were
all getting a little tired of his using this nickname so
often lately. "Yes, Ben, we know."

"Birdsong Trail, then?" said Dad. He looked at
each of us in turn for agreement, his eyes finally
resting on me. I nodded.

Mom looked young, almost girlish in her blue
jeans and sneakers, which she hardly ever wore. As
she was fishing her sunglasses out of her purse, she
cried, "Oh, no. I don't believe it!"

I was the first one to reach her side. "What's the
matter?"

"I can't go!" she said, holding up an appointment
card from the doctor. "I have my annual physical,
which I scheduled three months ago."

"What's a physical?" Ben wanted to know.

"It's an exam at the doctor's," I explained to Ben.
Then to Mom, I said, "Can't you change it? Please?"

"No, I can't. I've waited three months for this

appointment, and anyway, they'd charge me for canceling on such short notice."

"What's short notice?" Ben asked.

"Ben," I objected, tired of his questions.

Coming up behind us, Dad replied, "That's when you don't call them in advance to give them time to get ready. Nell, we'll go after your appointment," he said, stroking her shoulder. "What time are you supposed to be at the doctor's?"

Looking sadly at the card in her hand, she shook her head. "Two o'clock. But I'm supposed to meet a woman from my Chinese art class at the exhibit downtown at four today. Well, there's no two ways about it, I can't go to Birdsong Trail," she finished, sighing. "But the rest of you can. I'll go with you another time."

"Please, Dad?" Ben begged. "Please let's go."

"Okay," he replied to Ben. "We'll miss you," he told Mom, giving her shoulder a squeeze. "Don't go turning any heads at the doctor's in those tight jeans of yours," he teased.

"Oh, Larry," she laughed, and I thought, *I hope that when I'm married a long time, my husband will still think I'm pretty, too.*

When we reached the park, I felt as if I had never been there before. Last time we came in the winter, the woods had a light, airy feeling because you could see right through the leafless trees. Every bird's nest was exposed to view, and many of the watering holes had been easy to reach since the vegetation around them had died back. Today, however, the undergrowth of the forest was returning to life and providing lots of hiding places for animals.

Last winter Ben and I had often wandered off the side of the trail on the soft cushion of leaves beneath the snow. But now so many plants grew there that I would never dream of stepping off the path for fear of destroying something living and beautiful. I noticed that my brother also stayed on the path.

*We are different, too,* I realized. *Last time Dad was absorbed in taking nature pictures; mostly, he wanted to be by himself for that. Ben raced back and forth like a puppy. I walked beside Mom, who was always looking ahead or behind us to make sure my brother was all right.*

*Alone,* I realized — *that's how I felt last time I was here. Alone in the cold woods, where everything was exposed.*

Today, however, the forest was thick with leaves and many singing birds, not just the twitter of chickadees. The trees seemed to lean over the path in welcome. Ben stayed with Dad and me, asking questions about unusual plants or animal holes before either of us even saw them.

I had to admit that walking beside Ben I noticed more, wondered about more things, and got more answers than if I had been by myself. I could see now why Dad called my brother Eagle Eyes; he seemed to take in the whole forest with a glance. Ben's excited comments drew out all the nature lore that Dad had been collecting since he was a boy, like the names of rare wildflowers, how to identify poison ivy, and which plants were edible. Aside from asking us to pose once or twice, my father hardly touched the camera around his neck.

Their conversation flowed around me like the warm breeze and birdsong, and I felt a part of my family and the forest beyond.

"Look, Emily, here's a huge fallen tree. Let's see how old it is," Ben called. As we bent over the stump, I felt a drop of rain splat on my back.

"Looks like a storm," Dad said, raising his head. "See those black clouds coming this way? We'd better head back to the car before we get wet."

Halfway there, the sky exploded with thunder and rain pelted down as if someone had turned on a very hard sprinkler. Dad laughed and put a guiding arm across each of our shoulders.

"Whew!" he said. "Guess this storm means business! Let's go," and we started to run as our clothes quickly became drenched.

As thunder crashed again, lightning ripped by — almost at the same moment.

"That was close," Dad said, suddenly becoming serious. As I took my eyes from the path for a second, Dad stumbled over a big rock beside the path and fell to the ground.

# I'm Somebody Too

"Come on, Dad," I said, taking his arm to help him to his feet.

I expected him to pull himself up and then tickle me or something, but he felt surprisingly heavy. "Help me, Ben," I said, still playful, tugging on his hand.

"No, give me a minute," my father said, wincing and rubbing his knee. Ben and I dropped his hands and stood waiting to see what he would do next.

Bracing himself on his arms, he struggled to his feet and attempted a step. He winced again. "Guess I really twisted my knee," he said, starting to ease himself back down to the ground. Suddenly he fell the rest of the way and took several deep breaths.

Fear gripped me. As I looked at my strong father sitting wet, dirty, and helpless on the ground, I realized that his leg hurt a lot more than he wanted us to know. Had he broken it? Would he ever be the same? Now, as the rain continued to soak us, the wet forest seemed menacing.

I shivered inside my wet clothes and recalled stories Dad had told us about hikers who were wet and got hypothermia. *People can die of just being outside in the cold, he'd said, if the temperature inside their bodies drops too low. But how will we get out of the forest if Dad doesn't lead us? Will anyone come to look for us in this storm? Suppose we get hypothermia sitting here and none of us can walk?*

"Come on, Dad, get up," Ben called, realizing that the game was over but not understanding how hurt

Dad was. "I'm cold and I have to go to the bathroom." He hopped from one foot to the other. "And I'm hungry too. It's starting to rain pretty hard, Dad. Let's..."

"Shut up, Ben," I interrupted. "Can't you see that he's hurt?"

"Emily, you're the oldest," said Dad, ignoring my rude comment. "You've got to go back to the ranger station and bring help."

"What ranger station, Dad?"

"Right where we parked our car," he replied.

The bleak, wet trees seemed to form solid walls on either side of us. "Which way is it?"

"*That* way, remember?" he replied somewhat impatiently. "That's the direction we were running before I fell. Just follow this path until you get to the next one and..." He scratched his beard. "Let's see. When you get to the next one...let's see... you take a left and then..."

Hopelessness filled me. *If he can't even tell me how to do it, what chance do I have of reaching the station?*

"I can do it, Dad," Ben broke in. "You just follow this path till you pass the old gate and stay on this trail till you cross the creek and turn at the signpost with the eagle on it," he said without taking a breath. "It's not far to the ranger station after that."

"Ben, I knew those eagle eyes of yours would come in handy," Dad replied. "You'll find the way just fine. Emily can stay here to keep me company." I sank gratefully to the ground beside him, not caring if I got mud on my jeans. I watched Ben speed down the trail as far as I could see him. As he rounded a bend, the gloomy forest seemed to swallow him.

The rain had stopped before he returned, but it didn't matter; Dad and I couldn't have gotten any wetter. I heard Ben before I saw him.

"We're almost there," he said excitedly to the man and woman who followed him, carrying a stretcher.

"Oh, no, you can't carry me," Dad objected when they reached us. "I'm too heavy."

"It's okay," the woman reassured him. "Some medics will be here in a minute to give us a hand. And thanks to this smart young man, who remembered your phone number, we were able to call your wife. Now, how's your leg?" she asked, kneeling beside him.

Suddenly my teeth began to chatter uncontrollably. "Pretty chilly out here, isn't it? This will warm you up," said the man, putting one blanket around me and the other around Dad.

By the time the medics carried Dad out of the woods, Mom was waiting in the parking lot with dry clothes for all of us. As Ben started to tell her all about Dad's accident, I fell asleep and stayed that way until we got to the hospital.

# Chapter 24

For the first time I could remember, all of us stayed home from church the next morning. I put on my Sunday clothes as usual, but at eight-thirty, when we usually had breakfast, Dad was still asleep. "Your father was awake most of the night after we got home from the hospital," Mom said, coming into my room still in her bathrobe. "I think I'll just let him sleep."

As Ben wandered in, she brightened. "Ben, Daddy told me how you saved the day yesterday, finding your way to the ranger station all by yourself. Thank you, honey."

Ben's whole face broke into a smile. "I was the only one who could do it," he replied. I glared at him for saying that, but he didn't even see me.

"That's what he told me. How did you know where to go? Dad said it was at least a mile, and you had to take more than one path," continued Mom.

"Oh, that was easy. We took that path last time we visited Birdsong Trail in the winter, and I noticed the eagle on the sign and the gate and the bird feeder. I have eagle eyes, remember?"

# I'm Somebody Too

Mom laughed. "You certainly do," she said appreciatively, ruffling his hair. "I'm so glad you were there to take care of Daddy and Emily."

*Take care of me?* I objected silently. *Isn't that pushing it a little too far? It was the rangers who gave me the blanket to keep me from getting hypothermia. All Ben did was help them find us.*

She looked fondly at me. "How are you this morning? Get enough sleep?"

I nodded crossly, for out of the corner of my eye I could see Ben throwing my unicorn-shaped eraser high up in the air and catching it. "Ben, give it back. You'll break off the horn," I objected.

Mom went out into the hall. "Let's get your medication, Ben," she said, putting the eraser on my dresser and closing my door. "Emily, you may change out of your dress. We're not going to church."

Dad came downstairs just in time for lunch. Afterwards, watching him limp carefully from chair to couch made me feel sluggish and heavy, too. "How is it, Daddy?"

"Sore and swollen," he replied. Pointing to the rain-soaked backyard, he said, "But at least I don't feel bad about not being able to go outside today," he said. "And," he added when he noticed Mom in the doorway, "I don't have to clean the garage." He grinned at her.

"Can I get you anything, honey?" Mom asked. "Magazines?"

"Yeah, I guess so," he replied. "Seriously, I hate to sit here doing nothing."

"Want to play checkers instead? Or cards?" I said hesitantly, knowing how much he liked to read about photography. *Well, at least I can ask,* I thought.

"Yeah, that would be great, Emily. Let's have a tournament."

Halfway through the game I got up to yawn and stretch. Without thinking, Dad started to do the same, then stopped, rubbing his knee. "Blasted thing," he murmured, shifting his leg on the couch and stretching only his upper body.

I felt restless, too. Hoping he wouldn't feel too bad if we quit our game, I said, "I'm sorry, Dad, but I think I've had enough." Suddenly his stretched-out figure seemed to fill the room and I felt like I couldn't breathe. I opened the back door for a little air.

Later that afternoon the phone rang and Mom answered it in the kitchen. It was Grandma. "Oh, that sounds like fun, Mamie, but I'm afraid we can't today. Larry dislocated his knee yesterday at Birdsong Trail and has to stay off it for a day or two till the swelling goes down."

"What did she want?" I asked after Mom hung up.

"She said there was a free concert at the mall and would we like to go."

I was tired of staying in the house on this rainy day. Without thinking, I said, "Just because Dad has to stay home, do we all have to?" Then, feeling disloyal, I blushed and covered my mouth. "I'm sorry, I didn't mean that."

From the couch in the other room, Dad spoke up. "That's okay, Emily, you're right. Maybe Mom would take you over to their house so you could go with them to the mall."

My embarrassment faded and happy excitement filled me instead. "Oh, do you think they would? That would be wonderful." I jumped up to call them, and soon it was all arranged. Ben was busy experimenting with the new paints Mom had given him for filling in his chart, so he stayed home.

After the short concert at the mall, Grandma and Grandpa took me out for ice cream and I filled them in on all the latest things I could do on horseback. Grandma bought me a new clip for my hair. When we got home, they came in to see how Dad was.

My father was still sitting on the same end of the couch where I had left him, and Ben was spreading new paintings across the table in front of him.

"Come see my paintings of Birdsong Trail, Grandma," Ben said. "See, here's the eagle I saw last winter catching a fish. I didn't see any this time. But there were two ducks yesterday — see?"

"Why, Ben, these are quite good," exclaimed Grandma. "I see you even painted the mallard's head green. Look, Ed," she said, beckoning to Grandpa.

"Ben, I didn't know you could paint," said Grandpa, bending over the paintings.

# I'm Somebody Too

"Ben has other hidden talents, doesn't he, Larry?" said Mom, offering chocolate chip cookies.

"You should've seen him yesterday, when I got hurt," said Dad to his parents, taking a hint from Mom. "We were at least a mile away from the car when I fell. The path took several turns before it reached the ranger station. So Ben had a lot to remember to get back to the station. But he found the way all by himself and brought help."

"I was the only one who could do it," Ben boasted.

"Why? I thought Emily was with you, too," asked Grandma, confused.

"She was too *scared*," said Ben.

"Ben..." warned Mom.

"But I was brave," he went on, ignoring her. "We were on that path last winter, and I saw *everything* then. You know, I have eagle eyes," he said, glancing at our grandparents.

"What are eagle eyes?" Grandpa asked.

"You know. Because I have ADD, I see everything, Grandpa — just like an eagle. I remembered, and I saved Dad and Emily."

I couldn't stand it anymore. "You *did not* save me! I would've been fine; I just needed a few minutes to rest. Besides, I talked to Dad the whole time to keep him from getting hypothermia. It was pretty cold sitting there on the ground. You all make me sound like a helpless idiot!"

"Emily, we didn't mean it that way," objected

Dad. "Of course I was glad to have you keep me company."

"Well, you never said so till now," I said hotly. "All you've talked about since we got home is Ben, Ben, BEN. Finding the ranger station is the first good thing he's ever done in his life, but I'm *always* good and you never say anything. I wish I had ADD!" I choked with tears, and in the stunned silence, fled out of the room.

"Let her go," I heard Mom say softly.

I grabbed my jacket and rushed out the door into the side yard. I wanted to fling myself onto the soft grass, but everywhere was wet, so I ran across the street and was soon in the woods near the golf course. As the cool wind stung my tear-streaked cheeks, I recalled the horrible scene I'd just made in front of everyone. Fresh tears came. I wandered blindly, knowing that I was safe here.

*I'm somebody too!* the angry face of the doll cried inside me. I knew it was that side of me who had spoken up in front of everyone. Giving myself over to the power of my anger, I ran into the wind, barely pausing when the uneven ground made me stumble. I ran as fast as any wild horse without a rider.

After a while my energy seemed to vanish suddenly, and I stopped, panting. Looking around for a dry place to sit, I spotted a big stump in a grove of trees protected from the wind. My legs felt heavy, but I dragged myself to my resting spot.

# I'm Somebody Too

Now that the angry me had had a chance to speak and run, I was filled with guilt. The other voice of the doll — the side with the smiling face — took over and started scolding me. *How could you let yourself carry on so? Your father is in pain and you're supposed to be nice and make everyone feel better like you usually do. Instead, you hurt the people you care about most — just like Ben.* I put my hands over my eyes and let the sobbing wash over me.

Then a new, more reasonable voice took over. *It's okay; they will understand. What you said was true; it's just too bad you had to say it now when things really have started to get better.* Then came the memory of how alive I felt walking beside Ben in the park. *He really isn't such a bad brother; in fact, lately he's been kind of fun,* the voice said. *And it was a good thing he found his way to the ranger station because you would probably still be lost in the woods or frozen in place.*

*Would it really hurt you that much to let him enjoy a little praise now and then?* the calm voice continued. *After all, everyone just smiled when he tried to make you sound like a helpless idiot. They know that you're dependable and hard working, loving, and loyal.*

*But Mom and Dad never said a thing about me!* the frowning side of me said. *They only noticed Ben, as usual.*

*They have said so many bad things to Ben in the past, they're just trying to make up for it now,* said the calm voice. *When you really think back, you can remember lots of times they thanked you for doing your homework or cleaning your room. And you got lots of hugs from Mom when you did something nice after Ben was particularly awful.*

I felt like a tight door was being opened into a small dark room. "Yes, that's true," I admitted aloud, glad that no one else was there to hear me say it.

Feeling greatly reassured by the calm voice, I took a couple of deep breaths and uncovered my eyes. My quiet moment suddenly shattered as Ben came charging toward me, yelling, "Here she is. I found her, Mom. She's right over there."

I was too far away to hear Mom's quiet instructions to him, but her gesture was clear. Taking Ben firmly by the arm, she pointed to the spot they were standing on, then walked on by herself. After a few seconds, Ben began to tag along behind her, but she turned and pointed to the same spot again. In spite of myself, I smiled. Ben's dancing in place reminded me very much of Mary's puppy. In many ways he was just as enthusiastic and lovable.

I got ready for my meeting with Mom by brushing my hair out of my eyes and taking another deep breath. *Will she be angry?* It didn't matter so much. I felt calm and strangely peaceful. *It's nice of her at least to save me the embarrassment of apologizing to Ben right away.*

"Emily, are you ready to come home now?" she called from a few feet away. Feeling suddenly shy, I nodded. Now she was beside me. I waited to see whether she would scold me for my outburst.

"Honey, what you said this afternoon made a lot of sense," she began. "We were so excited about Ben's pulling himself together to help your father that I guess we kind of exaggerated it. But you know, I *have* been telling you lately how much I appreciate and love you. So has Daddy. Sometimes, though, I think you don't even hear me; you're so busy comparing yourself to Ben.

"Emily, you and Ben are both so special to me. The love I have for you is very different from my love for him. You never have to worry that my loving Ben takes anything away from you, because it's not the same kind of love." Putting her arm around me, she said, "Emily-love is special."

I had heard her say many things like that before. This time, however, I was able to believe her because her words echoed the new, calm voice inside me that said the same thing.

# Chapter 25

Several days later it looked like Ben was taking the two steps backwards that Dr. Lawson had warned me about — and all of us suffered with him. I was supposed to get my hair trimmed after school, but Ben missed the bus home.

As soon as I walked in the front door, Mom said, "Come on, Emily, we have to go get Ben at school." Then after dinner, Ben announced that he had a big test on his times tables. He worked on them until after his bedtime — first with Dad, then with Mom. Hearing him make all those mistakes was so frustrating that I went to my room and shut the door.

"But I don't know them yet!" I heard Ben cry in the kitchen below. Dad said something I couldn't catch, then Ben protested loudly, "I have to know them all for tomorrow or I'll flunk third grade."

He was climbing the stairs now, with Mom close behind him. "You need your sleep, Ben. You've done all you can tonight." She sounded drained.

"But Mom, I'll flunk third grade!" he repeated in the same whiny voice. *This is going to turn into a big argument any minute, just like old times.* Part of me wanted to run out there and make it all right, but I knew I couldn't. Shutting myself in my room, I covered my ears with my hands. Humming loudly, I tried to distract myself by thinking hard about what to wear to school tomorrow. *Maybe I'll braid my hair like an old-fashioned girl.*

Finally all was quiet outside my door and I ventured out. Mom was tucking in Ben for the night. "I have a sore throat," he said.

"I'll get you a throat lozenge," she said tiredly, and padded on slippered feet to the hall closet. After rummaging there for a few minutes, she came into my room, where I was laying out my clothes.

"Emily, where are the throat lozenges? I just bought a whole bag last week. They can't be gone yet."

"I didn't take them all, Mom, honest," I replied.

Ben came to the door of his room then, shifting nervously from one foot to the other. "Me neither."

*Uh-oh,* I thought. *She hates it when she accuses us of doing something and neither of us admits to it. She'll surely lose her temper now.*

Mom took a deep breath, and her voice was louder than usual when she said, "I don't care who did it, and I'm not trying to blame anyone. I just want you to know those things are not candy. I buy them for when you have sore throats, and that's the only time you're to eat them."

"They taste awful, Mom. I would never eat them

for candy," Ben assured her. Mom nodded, then looked to me for an answer.

"Well, I did take a few," I admitted, adding hastily, "But I do have a sore throat, Mom; it's been sore for lots of days. I just didn't want to bother you." Ben shot me a grateful look and wandered back to his room.

Mom's angry face and voice disappeared as if washed away by her concern for me. Inwardly I breathed a sigh of relief.

"Emily, you should tell me when things are bothering you instead of keeping them inside. Especially after you've had strep throat. Does it hurt like last time?" She ran her hand gently down the side of my face and throat as if to brush the soreness away. I leaned against her palm.

"No, it doesn't hurt that bad, and it's just at night. I would tell you if it got bad again."

"Good." She patted my cheek and returned to the medicine closet. After rummaging for a moment, she returned with the green throat spray. "Maybe this will help. Open up," she said.

Obediently I stuck my tongue out as far as it would go. Mom had a terrible aim, so I had to make it as easy as possible for her to squirt the back of my throat rather than my tongue. She had to do it twice before it found its mark.

Ben was dancing around in my doorway. Mom looked up irritably. "You're supposed to be in bed, Ben. Oh, well, let me spray your throat, as long as you're up," she said, raising the bottle in his direction. Sticking out his tongue as far as he could, he also scrunched up his eyes, making a terrible face — worse than the ones he used to make when he was trying to get her mad.

She paused, looking at him for a moment as if trying to decide whether he was being disrespectful. I held my breath. *Not now, Mom, please don't make a scene just before bed.* Dad came up the stairs and stood quietly at the top. *He's just as worried as I am,* I realized.

Suddenly she dropped her arm and started to laugh — not one of those polite, breathy laughs; not a sarcastic, bitter laugh; but a real laugh. Tears streamed down her cheeks. Ben's eyes flew open and he sucked his tongue back into his mouth, surprised.

"You should have seen your face!" she gasped finally, wiping her eyes. "Ahhh," she mimicked him, scrunching up her face and sticking her tongue out.

I couldn't believe it — my mom, who was always so serious and so concerned about getting everything right, kneeling on the floor and acting like an idiot. Dad tickled her to hear her make that beautiful sound again, and Ben and I made bug eyes and ugly faces to do our part. After her almost-explosion, it felt so good to be silly.

When we'd all settled down again, Mom sprayed Ben's throat and kissed him. Dad guided him gently to bed, where he went without a struggle.

# I'm Somebody Too

"Good night, Squirt," he said to Ben.

"I'm not Squirt," I heard Ben protest. "I'm Eagle Eyes, remember? Oh, you were joking about squirting my throat. Dad, can I look at the stars through my telescope? It's clear tonight."

"No, it's late and you need your sleep," Dad said firmly, clicking off the lamp. "Good night."

I returned to my room, where Mom was plugging in the vaporizer, waiting to tuck me in. "You'll be fine in the morning," Mom said softly.

"I know," I said, believing her with all my heart. The vaporizer gurgled.

The darkness in my room felt moist and friendly as my parents walked down the hall together, clicking off the light at the top of the stairs. Tonight there would be no bad dreams; Ben, Mom, and Dad were okay, and so was I.

As my parents started down the stairs, Dad said softly to Mom, "What came over you tonight, Silly? I think I just saw the sparkling eyes of the woman I married." When I heard her answering giggle, I sighed with deep satisfaction and drifted off to sleep.

§§§

# *Epilogue:*
# *Surviving the Storm*

If you're like Emily, sometimes your fear and anger seem strong enough to carry you away. Although it is normal to feel this way, emotions can't really do that. Try some of these remedies the next time you're upset.

• Breathe deeply. Often when we become angry or frightened, we don't breathe very much. However, you will be able to relax and think more clearly if you pause and take big, deep breaths. Count to five as you inhale, pause a few seconds, and exhale as long as you possibly can. Do this several times.

• Take a walk and groan out your anger, saying things like, "Ohhh, my parents don't care about me. Ohhh, I got a failing grade. Ohhh, I always have to do all the work." After awhile, switch to "I'm happy because..." and mention all the good things you can think of.

• Let out your bad feelings by kicking a ball, running, doing pushups, or pounding your pillow or bed. Or take a big sheet of paper and crayon and scribble hard and fast, choosing angry colors. When you have finished, tear the paper into tiny shreds.

• Keep an "Anger Journal". Write, "I'm angry at (person's name) because...."

• Keep a "Worst Possible Situation Journal". Draw a line down the middle of the page. On the left side, write, "The thing I fear most is...because...." On the right side, list what you would do if the bad thing occurred or reasons you think it won't ever occur.

• Find a trustworthy adult with whom you can discuss these disturbing feelings. (This is especially important if you think something scary really will happen.) If you wish, you may show him or her the journals mentioned above. Or talk to someone your own age who will keep your conversation private.

• Remind yourself that you are more than your feelings. Say to yourself, "The feeling of anger (or fear) is passing through me now."

• Close your eyes and imagine your bad feelings floating away like a helium balloon. Exhale deeply as you picture them drifting farther and farther away, finally vanishing from your sight.

§§§

# About the Author

In *I'm Somebody Too,* Jeanne Gehret weaves memories of her own childhood into more recent experiences with her husband and two children. She frequently joins her family for a sled ride on the golf course near their home in Fairport, New York, and has many photos of them feeding chickadees by hand at Birdsong Trail. While writing this novel, she learned to ride horseback and make French braids. Despite the similarities between her family and Emily's, the author insists that the people and events in this novel are fictitious.

§§§

## *Also by Jeanne Gehret:*

### *Picture books for ages six to ten*
- Eagle Eyes: A Child's Guide to Paying Attention
- The Don't-give-up Kid and Learning Differences

### *Coming soon:*
New audiotape for parents
of youngsters with ADD

### *Author visits*
may be arranged by calling the publisher.
Or write for our "Unforgettable Author Visits"
brochure for more details.

**Verbal Images Press**
19 Fox Hill Drive • Fairport, New York 14450
(716) 377-3807 • Fax (716) 377-5401